Demon Trouble Too

Demon Guardians

Book 2

TERRY SPEAR

DEDICATION

Dedicated to readers of urban fantasy who love the unusual—the underdog, the misunderstood, the paranormal characters who are really the good guys.

ABOUT DEMON TROUBLE TOO:

Alana Fainot is a demon gate guardian, stuck in her last boring year of school. But not for long. Hunter and the rest of the gang show up when her astral form can't return to her physical form, and she's at the police station trying to talk her way out of having seen the murderer of a summoner. Hunter always knew Alana was trouble, but his kind of trouble, and he's not leaving Alana alone again.

Celeste Sweetwater, a new kind of demon, joins Hunter and Alana and the rest of the demon guardians in a fight to find a new kind of portal device that can summon several demons at once. But not only that, another Matusa has been unleashed on the unsuspecting human world and the demon guardians must stop him before he wreaks much more havoc.

But this time, the police are involved, paranormal investigators pounce on the area, and the whole mess seems to be spiraling out of the demon guardians' control.

PROLOGUE

The storms over Baltimore sucked every centimeter of light out of the sky. No starry bodies twinkling across an ebony velvet night. No glimpse of a moon, even the hint of a new moon's shadowed existence. Only masses of black clouds blanketing the city, the air heavy with wet moisture, the threat of rain hanging gloomily all about her.

In black jeans and the same colored sweatshirt and sneakers, Celeste ran toward the zoo, heard a lion roaring on the stiff wind, felt the stormy turbulence circling her. She had to get away from the man and woman and their bratty daughter whom she called... *no*, she didn't call family. Some foster parents she'd heard were good, who would provide a loving home for children who needed them.

She didn't want the ones she'd been stuck with this time. They certainly didn't need her. The fault was not all theirs, she had to admit. She'd always been difficult.

She couldn't help it. Seeing visions in her head of things to come made her too weird for them to handle. For any of the foster parents she'd lived with over the years since she was three, she'd found it was the same story. She wasn't about to hide what she saw. Although her foster parents and the social workers who placed her in their homes insisted she not speak of what she envisioned.

Why should she hide what haunted her in the form of nightmares and day terrors? Why should she have to hold it all in?

Schizophrenia, paranoia, oh yeah, any neat term they could call it, that's what doctors labeled her mental state, just because they couldn't subscribe to the notion that psychics existed.

But the visions had gotten worse and tonight, she wanted to run away from what she'd envisioned—a Matusa demon killing a human—and from the family who refused to believe she saw them. She wanted to get away from all of it as far as humanly possible. Yet, how could she? When she wasn't even human?

She meant to run away from the visions, and yet as before, she was racing straight into the face of terror as if she had no power over her own feet. As soon as she reached the gates at the zoo, she saw blue-green lights spreading outward at the edges in a 3-dimensional sphere, expanding, more oblong than circular. Glittering in the Baltimore night, beckoning her, the portal willed her to find a way into the zoo and seek the light, as if she was dead and she needed to find peace in heaven.

She knew to run far away and hide from the portal that had opened the thin fabric between the demon world of Seplichus and Earth world. Knew that one of the Dark Ones could be drawn forth as well as any number of different kinds of demons. But if it was a Dark One and he saw her standing there, he could even think she'd summoned him forth, and then she'd be dead. Maybe not immediately. Maybe he'd make her suffer first for having the audacity to call him forth to do her bidding.

But then again, wouldn't he realize she wasn't human at all? That she had no way to summon a demon? At least she didn't think she could. She had no interest in trying, either. Who knew what she'd pull out of the hat?

Then again, she could hide her demon aura. And so she did.

Since *she* had not opened the portal, someone else had, and he or she had to be nearby. If the summoner saw her transfixed to the spot, he might even think she was the demon he had summoned forth. The one he would think he could enslave.

Which meant, she had to get away. So, why was she searching for a way *into* the zoo?

Because, as long as she could remember, she was always trying to find a way to control the outcome of a vision. Not only that, she couldn't quite decide what it was, but it was almost as if she was drawn to peril. She shook her head at the notion.

She ran along the fence, attempting to locate a way in as if she was one of the caged animals desperately seeking a way out. Her brain screamed at her to fight the urge compelling her to head in this direction, but her heart—that was pounding out of control—didn't want her to, either.

For years, she'd been shuffled from one family to another after her summoner parents had been murdered by one of the Matusa demons, through their own folly. If they hadn't brought him forth, they most likely would still be alive. She snorted. They'd wanted a baby brother for her. Bringing her over had been easy. Bringing him—a full grown Matusa—into this world had been a fatal mistake.

She found a break in the fence—no, not a break, but a place where someone had physically cut through the chain link, which should have warned her away. She wriggled inside, then dashed back through the exhibits where she'd observed the portal. When she saw the shimmering lights, she came to a dead halt. If she hadn't seen what had happened to her parents—or the ones who had made themselves her parents—she wouldn't fear what she saw before her now.

She was both terrified and mesmerized. How could part of her desire to step through the portal and see what the demon world looked like? When part of her knew better?

She wasn't of that world.

She was different. Yes.

But she hadn't been raised there. Wouldn't it be worse than moving from lush green Oregon, to the scrub brush strewn lands of western Oklahoma? And then to the city of Baltimore?

Of course it would. Because demons ruled the world in Seplichus. And she wasn't one of them.

She wasn't.

How could she be? She hadn't a clue as to what their world would be like. What their people were like. She wouldn't be any more accepted there than she was here.

She scoffed at herself as she walked toward the portal, knowing she shouldn't take another step closer. *Not one more step.*

That's when the portal collapsed inward and a screech of shocking proportions ripped through the air.

Shaken, her heart beating a million miles a minute, Celeste ran away from the disintegrating portal and the horror trapped within.

CHAPTER 1

Alana Fainot slumped at her desk in calculus class, Day One, hating that she had to be here when she was probably needed to save the world. *Somewhere.*

Certainly, advanced math was not required in her line of work. Most of all, she hadn't wanted to return to *Baltimore* to her old high school to complete her senior year. Her mother had insisted she leave her uncle's home in Dallas to return to live with her. Normally, Alana would have been bemoaning the fact she had to stay with her neat-nick uncle for any length of time.

Everything had changed once she had learned she was half Kubiteron demon, not just a witch, and that she had a mission—keep the demons from entering the world when a portal was called forth by some clueless human.

She still wasn't really fond of the idea that she had to guard the gates and send the demons back, particularly when the nasty-tempered Matusa entered. They were dangerous and most of the time deadly, and she really didn't think she could deal with one strictly on her own.

Which was another reason she hated returning to Baltimore.

She'd had to leave Hunter Ross behind. Half Matusa and half pain in the butt, he was a first-class demon hunter. As much as she hated to admit that she needed anyone, she needed him. Well, his protection when it came to dealing with Matusa. Not that she couldn't deal with them in part. But she really needed him at her side when she did. She tried to tell herself that was the only reason she couldn't quit thinking about him.

She couldn't stop thinking about Jared Kensington, either. He was a lesser demon in the pecking order in the demon world, a full-blooded Elantus that were usually pretty good-natured. So she'd heard.

Except when it came to her. She outranked him in demon order, but was a less powerful demon than Hunter. Every demon was less powerful than a Matusa.

Jared still believed she'd be the death of Hunter, and so he'd held a major grudge against her. Although sometimes he riled Hunter by showing he really cared for Alana, more in a girlfriend/boyfriend way. Not that Alana was buying it, either. She figured it was more of a way of his causing trouble between her and Hunter.

To her amusement, it did. Was Hunter jealous? Nah. He couldn't be.

The two of them weren't the only reason she didn't want to return to Baltimore though.

She hated it here because she was the only witch in the whole school. Courtesy of being only half witch. Because she was also half demon. So, she really didn't fit in. She hadn't really been working on her witch's spells like she should have been, either, resenting that she wasn't all human. Until she discovered that that wasn't the only problem she had. How many kids her age could claim half demon heritage? Two that she knew of. Hunter and her.

Then she had the problem with being pulled to portals opening when humans, sometimes warlocks or witches, summoned demons into their world. She was drawn to them in a really weird way—teleported in mind, body, and soul, kind of. Yet, she wasn't physically there. Except everyone saw her there. And she could even speak to them. Talk about weirding everybody out, including herself.

Just chalk it up to being really bizarre. The good thing was no one could hurt her in her astral form. The bad part was that sometimes the demon came looking for her afterwards if she had witnessed something—like murder—that he didn't want announced to the whole wide world. Not that she'd be dumb enough to tell the world that she'd witnessed a demon murder his summoner. How dumb did a Matusa think she could be?

Oh, and yeah, then she had this other slight problem. All demons were attracted to the Kubiteron females. Like she had some kind of pheromones that called out to the male demons, saying, *I'm interested if you are.* Only

3

she wasn't. And it really ticked her off that she couldn't control that aspect of herself.

Which, in circumspect was probably another reason Jared sometimes acted as though he liked her. She had this automatic demon perfume designed to get their attention. Even if deep down, he didn't want to have anything to do with her.

But right now, she was stuck in calculus class. Not only had her mother insisted she leave her uncle's home in Dallas, but he had also. She suspected he couldn't deal with all the trouble she'd brought to his home. Demons were real. She was a bona fide half demon. Yep. She'd turned his whole world upside down. Since he was a high-level warlock, not much did. In his methodical way, he was probably still trying to come to terms with it.

So he insisted she return to live with her mother and finish her senior year at high school. What a waste of time. What was she going to do with learning calculus or chemistry? Not when she needed to improve her witch's skills every waking hour and learn whatever other abilities her demon half could contribute to her guardian duties.

She needed an arsenal of weapons if she was to make a stand against the Dark Ones when they left the demon world and came here.

As soon as she took her seat, way in the back of the class, she felt the ghostly chill of the dead Matusa, Indigo, as he settled at the empty desk next to her. He gave her one of his cock-eyed evil smiles. She shook her head at him. He had *promised* not to bother her at school. She should have figured he'd lie. *Matusa demon.*

She wondered how long he'd sit in class and behave himself. Not for long, she imagined.

What really stoked her ire was when Ferengees Samson, though he insisted on being called Samson, walked into the class. His blond hair curled about his ears and his green eyes took in everything around him. As soon as he spied her, he headed for the desk next to hers. One thing about Samson, he had a nice round face that always made him look rather jovial. Or almost always jovial. She usually was too busy fighting a demon to know what his expression was when he was battling his own. Or he wasn't quite all there. He had a peculiar way of turning into mist when a battle arose.

Still, she stared at the Samuria demon in disbelief to see him here. She had warned him *not* to come to class. She didn't want him saying something that couldn't be easily explained since he was all demon and had never lived in the human world. Luckily, he looked like most anyone else in class, jeans, sneakers, well, except for the golfing shirt. He thought they were cool.

Hunter had vehemently told him he wasn't to hang around her any longer also. Not that Samson listened to Hunter all that much. And certainly, now that Hunter was miles and miles away in Dallas, Samson really wasn't listening to the Matusa. But even so, being a half Matusa, Hunter expected to be obeyed. They were the most evil and powerful of demons, after all. But his human half tempered his gruffer personality and his growl was often worse than his bite. At least with her. Most of the time.

Samson believed he was to be her protector, paired with her for life because she was a gate guardian. She didn't agree. Neither did Hunter.

Jared, on the other hand, was all for it. Although she was often at odds with the electronic genius, a full-blooded Elantus demon, she missed him, too. Or maybe not him, exactly, but his laptop that warned them when a demon was in the area. He was working on a demon tracker device that would be as small as a cell phone, easy to carry, and each of them could have one as an early warning system.

As loyal as Jared was to Hunter for saving his life, Jared was making one of the trackers for him first. Then he'd make a portable one for himself. And lastly, for her. Samson wasn't on the list of customers because Hunter wouldn't let him be.

Alana was a more powerful demon than Jared, she had reminded him. *And* she was a witch. To her way of thinking, she should get a device before *he* did. But he wasn't listening to her. Particularly when he and Hunter were in Dallas and so far away. Otherwise, she figured she would have been able to browbeat one out of Jared after Hunter had his own.

The teacher walked into class and began taking roll call. Alana must not have heard the bell ring, her thoughts still on Jared and his mini-demon tracker devices. Too bad he couldn't sell the invention to a company that could mass market them. Then again, except for their little group of four demon hunters, she didn't figure anyone else would have any use for them.

Indigo was moving about the students seated in class, doing his ghostly best to freak them out as he sifted from desk to desk, chilling them with his presence. Thankfully, he wasn't doing much more than that. Not until he saw Alana observing him, and then as if wanting to really show her what he could do, he smiled in his dark way and headed straight for the teacher.

Oh... my... God... no!

No one could see the ghostly entity like Alana could. Well, and like her mother could, ghost buster that she was. He was dark-haired, like most of the Matusa she'd encountered, except his hair was jet black. His hair was cropped short though, and he had the look of a biker dude—leather pants, leather jacket, black T-shirt, black boots. She hadn't been able to see him before when he'd come to their aid, but she figured he'd become more comfortable with being around her. He had both the aura of a Matusa, which helped her to define what type of demon he was, and a ghostly silhouette that indicated he was not of this world.

He was handsome, as all Matusa were. Deadly handsome, with a rugged face, not an ounce of extra flesh—looked to be an athletic type, tall, muscled, a regal nose, and a haughty expression that screamed arrogance. Arrogant, as were all Matusa.

Hunter included.

On edge, Alana watched, unable to make Indigo cease and desist. No matter how many times she'd tried to exorcise him so he wouldn't be floating around Earth world causing trouble, she hadn't managed it. It seemed to her that even in death, a Matusa with a grudge— another had murdered him to claim power over the area—was still a powerful presence.

The teacher, Mrs. Cogsworth, was catching students up on simple math they'd probably forgotten over the summer, writing on the board while Samson was taking studious notes. Mrs. Cogsworth was totally unaware that Indigo was standing beside her, mimicking her in his silent ghostly way.

Alana shook her head. As long as he didn't do anything more… *no… no… no…*

He began to pick up one of the markers and, of course, all anyone else could see if they were watching her was the red marker waving in the air near the teacher. The cap came off. Then the marker was pressed against the white board and started drawing.

Alana glanced at the students. Some were watching as the unsmiley face suddenly appeared about a foot away from the teacher, who was oblivious. Alana wondered if he hated math. The students, who were watching Indigo, stared at the paranormal occurrence in silent horror. What if the marker targeted them next? That's what she would have been thinking had she not been able to see Indigo and know him somewhat. Although she probably would never truly *know* him.

Unable to do anything about him and his ghostly actions, she glanced again at Samson. He was so absorbed in the teacher's explanations, he didn't even see Indigo's drawing.

Did the demons teach calculus in the village where Samson was from? Somehow, she hadn't really envisioned him as the studious type.

He interrupted the teacher with so many pointed questions, indicating he was way ahead of probably most of the students in math, if not all, that Mrs. Cogsworth finally asked him to hold his questions until the end of the class. But Alana could tell that her teacher was pleased that someone was interested in her lecture.

When she turned her back to him and began writing some more equations on the board, Samson smiled at Alana as if to show her just how smart he was. Was she impressed?

She mouthed, "Show off."

He grinned and watched the teacher some more, turning his head only slightly to see the unsmiley face on the board. Samson said to Alana in a whisper, "*Indigo?*"

She nodded.

Samson shook his head. Since Alana had returned to Baltimore, the ghosts that the Matusa had stirred up were wreaking havoc at a much more acceptable level. Her mother was back to taking care of the hauntings that arose on her own. Although Alana would rather ghost bust or fight the evil demons and free the enslaved ones any day over the drudgery of school.

She noticed that several of the students were playing games on cell phones on their laps, others drawing pictures, or writing notes. Not the math kind. Indigo had slipped out of the room, probably annoyed he wasn't getting any really great response from anyone over his unsmiley face or chilling everyone by thirty degrees or more.

Only Samson seemed intrigued with the teacher's lecture. That's when Alana noticed an older girl who seemed inordinately interested in Samson. She looked like she must have been held back a couple of years.

Maybe she was one of those math whizzes and liked him because he was also and that he wasn't afraid to show it. Or maybe she was so bad in math, she was looking at Samson as a tutor after hours. Alana would give anything if Samson could find someone else to… well, maybe date, so he'd quit telling her she was his intended mate.

Maybe in the demon world it would have been the case. But she wasn't all demon. And so that meant whatever he thought the protocol was for demon gate guardians and bodyguards who watched over them didn't count in this case. Right?

Alana prayed he wouldn't tell anyone at school that she was his intended mate!

The girl was beautiful and had a sophisticated look, unlike Alana who thought of herself more in a sporty way. The girl was wearing a black dress, more suited to going to an evening dressy kind of party and didn't fit in with the jeans crowd.

The more she observed the girl, the more the hair prickled on the nape of Alana's neck. She didn't know what it was about her, but something wasn't quite right.

Samson was totally unaware that anyone else was watching him. He was too engrossed with the teacher's lecture that Alana imagined if she walked out of the class right now, he wouldn't even notice.

She used her witch's ability to ensure the teacher didn't realize she was leaving the class and left. She was headed for the water fountain at the other end of the hall when she heard footsteps behind her and turned.

Samson. So he *was* watching her after all. "Why are you out here? You're missing all those notes you should be taking," she said, teasing him.

"Why are *you* out here? You're missing the teacher's lecture. It's your school, your class." He was serious, as usual.

"You can teach me all you know later."

He shook his head. "This is the easy stuff like adding one and one and getting two."

"I know that, Samson. I mean, when the math gets harder and if I don't understand it, you can help me then. Why are you taking notes, if you already know all this stuff?"

He shrugged. "Someone ought to look like the teacher's effort is worthwhile."

She smiled. He was still a big mystery to her, but she loved how considerate he could be of others at times.

"You must be a genius."

He looked inordinately pleased that she'd compliment him. She didn't mean it that way. She had to be careful with any praise she offered him as he immediately concluded she was rethinking the mate scenario.

Indigo hurried to join them, and Samson quickly chided, "Did you *have* to invite him?"

Their breaths were frosty, and she assumed that's why Samson knew Indigo had suddenly arrived. "When do I *ever* invite him? He does his own thing. By the way, did you notice the girl who was admiring you in class?"

"I only have eyes for you," he insisted, his green eyes growing dark with interest.

She groaned and headed back to class. "I think she likes that you're so smart in math," she tried again. Maybe that some other cute girl found his abilities noteworthy would make him lighten up some with Alana.

That's when she felt the compelling surge of a portal opening somewhere in Baltimore, and her heartbeat sped up. She grabbed Samson's hand to keep herself upright, and said between gritted teeth, hating that this was happening now but having no choice to avoid its pull, "Portal opening. Astral transporting time."

"Evil demon or good?" he hurriedly asked, his expression more worried than she'd ever seen it.

She was gone before she could reply.

CHAPTER 2

Samson wondered just how long it would be before Alana realized they were meant to be together, permanently. He knew it was just a ploy that she was trying to foist him off on getting interested in some other girl in class. A human? No way.

He was glad that Alana liked that he was smart. He wasn't certain she'd appreciate that fact. But he wanted to tell her how fortunate she was to have teachers and all the fantastic subjects humans could learn. Where he was from, teachers taught reading and writing and that was it. For anything more than that, he had to find teachers in the city, willing to educate him in other topics. He couldn't understand her dismissal of all she had here, when he wanted to sign up for every course the high school offered. Instead, he'd have to use his ability to vanish and visit more of the interesting classes, if he didn't have to watch over Alana. *Like now.*

He was torn between taking her out to her car until she could return to her physical form, or guide her into the class and make her sit in her seat before the bell rang. But she was like a zombie, unable to respond to anything anyone said, so he just wasn't sure what to do with her.

When he'd trained to be a gate guardian's bodyguard, no one had said anything about having to protect a half human. Well, half witch. Not that she wasn't human, too. She was just witchier than them.

He opted for taking her back to class. And hoped he wasn't making a big mistake. Indigo must have taken off with Alana's astral form because the hallway had warmed up by several degrees. If Samson could exorcise him, he would do it with a snap of the fingers. But for now, he hoped that Indigo could watch out for Alana wherever she'd gone. He prayed she'd return soon before anyone noticed she wasn't really all here.

***

Hunter had been searching for demons in Dallas for three days now and had sent one back, but found no others, while Jared worked on creating the Demon-Tracker II device. The city was relatively quiet, and he should have been glad. But he couldn't be. Not when he'd left Alana behind.

Jared's adoptive parents had put him up in a two-bedroom apartment, feeling that he needed to be on his own now. Which suited him fine. Hunter had moved in and the two were free to continue taking care of demons until they could discover how to eliminate the way portals were being opened. But it was a mixed bag of good and bad.

Jared denied he really cared whether he could ever find his biological demon parents, but every free chance he got, he returned to the demon world of Seplichus to search for them at the hall of records. Despite the animosity Hunter felt toward his own demon father, Bentos, not ever having wanted to meet him, he *was* his flesh and blood father. So sealing off the portals forever would mean burning their bridges to the demon world. And Hunter wasn't certain he wanted to do that.

Not only that, but Alana's father slipped back and forth between worlds also.

Ever since Hunter had left Alana behind in Baltimore, he'd felt out of sorts, unable to focus on his mission. He knew she had the hots for him, no matter that she tried to deny it. What bothered him most was that Samson so firmly believed that he was the one who would have Alana as his mate because of the gate guardian nonsense.

Not that her *job* was nonsense, just that the notion that Samson would believe his claim to her was.

Hunter had warned Samson to stay away from her, though he knew the Samuria wouldn't. He had done so as more of a warning that Samson was to keep his hands off, rather than to stay far away from her. In truth, the Samuria could protect her when Hunter was too far away to do so. That was what really griped him.

Then Frosty the ghost had designs on her also.

Hunter was clueless as to how to deal with Matusa ghosts though. Just as Hunter had suspected when he'd first seen her in her astral form, she was trouble. The kind he loved. As much as he told himself otherwise.

In the living room, he sat staring at Jared's laptop, trying to focus on anything, but envisioned only Alana's bright green eyes staring back at him, a determined look on her face, arms crossed. Beautiful.

He glanced at his watch. She was still in school. Would be for hours. He wished she could telepathically communicate with him like she could when she was close by and let him know if she was in trouble. But she couldn't from this distance.

What difference would it make anyway? He'd never get there in time to save her if she ran into something dangerous she couldn't deal with.

He glanced up as he heard footfalls coming toward the living room.

Jared stalked toward him, his face grave, and he handed Hunter his phone.

He knew from the look on Jared's face it was the worst kind of news. But *why* would anyone call *Jared* about it? And *who* would be calling him about it?

"Hello?" Hunter snapped, unable to contain his worry that something might have happened to Alana, yet he knew whoever the caller was it couldn't have anything to do with her.

"She's mine," the baritone male voice growled, and the line disconnected.

Hunter was already on his feet and headed for the bedroom. "Who was it?" he asked Jared.

"How do I know?" he asked, throwing up his hands in resignation. "I don't read minds. I didn't recognize the voice."

"Pack light." Hunter stormed into his bedroom and grabbed a backpack. "What did he say to you?" he hollered as Jared moved around in his own room.

"Just 'Hunter,' as if I was some damned secretary for you."

Hunter couldn't help smiling at that. Then he sobered and shoved enough clothes for five days in the pack.

"Where are we going?" Jared asked, from down the hall still.

"Baltimore."

"She might not be in trouble."

"When is the Kubiteron *not* in trouble?" Hunter growled.

"Yeah, you're right. She's trouble. I've always said so. I'm taking two bags, Hunter. Well, three."

"I said pack light."

Jared joined Hunter in the living room and handed him one of them. "You can carry my laptop."

Hunter stared him down for a moment before eyeing the other bags. When did an Elantus demon believe he could have a Matusa carry his bags for him?

"I'm bringing the Demon Tracker IIs with me so I can finish them up while you watch over Alana. Only two bags allowed per person on the plane. We don't want this stuff to go into baggage claim."

"Who was he?" Hunter asked, whipping out his keys to the pickup. Jared could carry his own bags until they had to board the plane. Maybe even carry them *on* the plane. But Hunter would store one of them for him underneath the seat in front of him.

"I swear I don't know."

"Any background noises to identify a location?"

They reached the truck and Hunter unlocked it while Jared paused to consider the question. Then he shook his head as he climbed into the truck and both buckled their seat belts. "No. Which was odd. No noise at all. Which, I guess isn't really that odd. But just makes it more difficult to identify where he was."

"Which means he doesn't want us to find him."

"Was he a Matusa?" Jared asked cautiously.

"Who else would go after her?"

Jared cleared his throat as they drove toward the airport.

Hunter sliced him a glower. "Besides any demon within breathing distance. You know what I mean. Which kind would dare call me and tell me he was laying claim to her?"

Jared sighed. "A Matusa. We still don't know for sure if this has anything to do with the Kubiteron."

"What other *she* do we know that someone would want?" Hunter snapped. He didn't mean to take it out on Jared. He was angry with himself for leaving her off in

Baltimore, knowing just how dangerous things could get if he wasn't there to watch her back. But her mother had really wanted her to finish her senior year in Baltimore, and her uncle had wanted that, too. No way could she have moved in with Jared and him.

Jared's cell phone rang, and he pulled it out of his pocket. "Hello, Samson?"

Hunter wanted to rip the phone away from Jared and speak to him himself, but he was pulling into long-term parking and needed to concentrate on getting parked and onto a plane, pronto. Still, it irritated him that Samson would call Jared, not him.

"I'll tell him. We're on our way. Yeah. *Really.* We're catching a flight out in another twenty minutes." He shoved the phone in his pocket as Hunter parked the truck.

"Why is he calling *you*?" Hunter asked, grabbing his bag.

Jared pulled out his three. "I'm easier to talk to." Jared gave him a quirky smile.

"You know that's not what I mean, Jared. What's wrong that Samson would call?"

"Alana's astral traveled. Samson was in class with her…"

Hunter gave him a dark look. Samson wasn't supposed to be in class with her.

Jared shrugged. "He was looking out for her. If he hadn't been, we wouldn't know what was going on now."

"So what's going on now?" Hunter led them toward the terminal for the Baltimore flight. "You did get us a flight, right?"

"Absolutely. Hacked into the online reservations. Bumped a couple of passengers. But I've paid for the seats, unlike Alana who sneaks her way on, using her witch's ability. We should be boarding in twenty minutes."

With Jared's keen abilities with computers, Hunter couldn't have hooked up with anyone who could be more useful in this business.

"So what's going on?"

"Alana hasn't returned to her physical form. Samson's pretty upset. He took her to two of her classes, and then when one of the teachers noticed how out of it she was, she wanted her taken to the nurse. He figured she suspected Alana was on drugs."

"Great."

"So he took her to a hotel."

"What?" Hunter's explosive response garnered several passengers' attentions.

"To keep her safe," Jared quickly said. "He was afraid to take her to her mother's condo. What if someone came for her there? But what's really spooked him is she hasn't returned to her physical body. Not only is it creepy when she's like that, *you know how it is*, but he's worried that somehow her astral self is being kept hostage. What if she can't return to her body if she's kept away from it for too long?"

Hunter cursed under his breath. "We're moving to Baltimore."

"What?"

"You heard me. Tell your parents first chance you get that we've got work in Baltimore. We'll need to cancel the contract on the other apartment and locate a place near where she goes to school. And you and I are going back to school."

"School?" Jared looked horrified. Then he gave Hunter one of his sarcastic smirks. "Yeah, you say you aren't hung up on the Kubiteron, but you've been moping for three days since we left her off in Baltimore. But I can't believe you want to go back to school just so you can watch over her. We graduated already! If my parents learn I'm going to senior year at high school again instead of starting college, they'll flip."

"They won't find out. She needs us. She's trouble, Jared," Hunter said, finding his seat on the plane. "She finds it and lures it to her location. Hell, we don't need tracking devices. All we need is her."

***

Alana was in one fine pickle of a mess, as her grandmother would say. Alana's father swore she'd get this astral plane traveling business under control someday. But no matter how much she had tried to learn how to break away from it and return to her physical body, she didn't have any real power over it.

Someone had opened the portal, but whoever had

done so was long gone. The blue and green lights were gone. The demon whoever the summoner had brought forth was gone. Just like last night. It had happened so quickly and so many times that she thought she had been dreaming. Now it was like it was happening all over again. Portal... no portal. And no one anywhere near it.

So here she stood in the middle of the zoo by the lion exhibit, no one seeing her, and no one for her to track down. She needed to find a summoner's book to destroy. But there was no summoner. And no minor demon to return to the demon world. Better yet, thankfully, no Matusa to have to deal with. She saw no sign of charred bodies or other violence, just a couple of sleepy lions watching her.

Hopefully no one would ask to see a ticket that proved she had paid to enter the zoo.

That's when she realized the zoo was devoid of people! It wasn't even open. Not this early in the morning. *Great.* If anyone saw her, she'd be toast.

How would she be able to explain she was really in school? *Physically.*

She *was* still in school, wasn't she?

Oh, poor Samson. He probably was beside himself concerning what to do with her. Too bad she couldn't be in two places at once. She hadn't been able to master such a thing yet. Her father had said given time, she might be able to. At least he could.

That wasn't happening for her either. At least for now.

A chill swept over her as she recalled more of what she'd thought had been a nightmare that she'd encountered during the night. She'd been here before, chasing blue-green portal lights as if they existed on an alien world. She remembered seeing... the African penguins at the Rock Island Penguin Habitat. And a reticulated giraffe. Even a hellbender in the Maryland Wilderness area. The huge salamander would slime its enemies when feeling threatened, but was also known as a snot otter and devil dog and was hiding under a rock when she'd seen it.

Or maybe she hadn't seen them in an astral teleportation. Maybe she'd only dreamt about them since she'd seen them in real life when she'd visited the zoo before.

So, why hadn't she remembered what had happened last night the first thing this morning?

Upon waking she'd forgotten what she'd seen in her dreams. Or had they been dreams? Had she been pulled in her astral form to an open portal, but been so sound asleep, she hadn't realized it was real?

The constant draw from one spot to another had been so unreal, so dreamlike that she couldn't imagine that it had been for real. She hadn't seen anything but the lights. No demons. No summoners. As soon as one portal evaporated, she had been pulled to a new location at the zoo to see a new portal, one by the cheetah exhibit, then another near the polar bear exhibit.

Bringing her fully aware she wasn't alone at the zoo,

a man shouted in an angry voice, "Hey, you there! We're closed! How'd you get in?"

Heart tripping, she turned to see a man wearing a maintenance uniform headed straight for her, looking peeved. She supposed she didn't appear like she could be any of the staff here, taking care of the animals. Not the way she was dressed in blue jeans, sneakers and a light pink T-shirt that had a large sparkly dark pink heart centered on it. When she'd learned she was half demon, she'd thought of wearing something more—demon-like. Particularly because she helped to rid Earth world of them, but also because she hunted ghosts and was half witch.

Black. Skulls. Angels with black wings. Dark, demonic.

But that was way too cliché. So she dressed as if she was an angel instead. Pink hearts. Sweetness and light. No demon would think her anything but an angel.

Right.

She watched the big man lumber toward her. She could speak now in her astral form, but if he tried to grab her, his hand would go right through her as if she was a movie projection. How weird would that be?

He would call the police. How would he explain what he'd seen?

If he didn't touch her, he could escort her outside of the zoo where she could wait for her mother to pick her up after he'd call her for Alana. She couldn't do such a thing. She'd need him to go back inside and not watch her. And she could just… vanish.

That wouldn't work. Her mother would come for her and Alana wouldn't be here. She was too far away to contact her mother telepathically, or she'd just do it that way. Her mother was on a job in Annapolis at the moment.

The chilling realization hit Alana. Why hadn't she returned to her physical form at school? When the portal closed, she was supposed to do that. Unless…

Another was open at the zoo somewhere nearby. Was someone thwarting her from feeling its compulsive draw?

The man towered over her, a hulking six-four she guessed, his hands on his hips. A big black mustache half covered his thin lips and looked like the other half had flown up his nose. "How did you get in here?"

"I… thought the zoo was open." She offered up some tears.

He wasn't falling for it. "The park's closed. Gate's closed. Ticket booth's closed. How did you get in here?"

"My mistake. I wanted to see the lions." She waved her hand at the lions, the male licking its paw, the lioness resting her head on her paws, snoozing.

"Come with me." He reached for her, but she quickly stepped back.

"I'm coming," she said, agreeably. He just couldn't touch her.

"Aren't you supposed to be in school?" he asked, glancing down at her, his look fierce.

"Home schooled," she lied. If her mother had been more patient with her, Alana would have asked her to homeschool her for her senior year. She wouldn't miss the parties or prom or any of that stuff. She wouldn't be asked out anyway.

And she'd only learn what she needed to. Who needed high school?

Then she felt the unmistakable draw of another portal being opened. *Oh, no... oh, no!*

She backed away from the maintenance man, so he wouldn't see her vanish in thin air, because that's exactly what she was about to do. Someone was summoning demons at the zoo. Why? Probably because it was so vacant right now.

The few staff that were here were probably busy taking care of the animals. Or like the maintenance worker, not able to be at all places at once.

"What the...," the man said in astonishment as she faded into oblivion.

But only for a second. She'd truly hoped she would have returned to her physical form, though that worried her, too. What had Samson done with her? She couldn't be sitting in classes like she was comatose. He must have taken her home.

Without wishing it, she was whisked away to another portal. Like the other, it closed just before she arrived. And there was no one there. No summoner. No portal. No demon. She was now by the exhibit housing the gorillas.

What was going on? It was like something was haywire, the portals appearing at random, but no one was summoning them, and no one was coming through them, either.

What if someone had developed a remote portal opener so he or she wouldn't have to be at the portal location when the demon came through? If it was a Matusa, the summoner would be safe. If the demon was one of the others, the summoner could pick them up later.

But no, there was no one here.

And didn't the summoner have to be at the portal to claim the demon right then and there, not later?

What if the summoner was only testing the device? And he hadn't worked out the bugs yet?

Then a more sinister thought came to mind. What if someone was messing with her personally? Was testing to see if summoning portals would pull her along like on a leash, bending her to his will? Ensuring she couldn't be at so many places at one time? So that the Matusa could enter the city unhampered? But couldn't they do that anywhere in the world? Why here? And why now? She was only *one* gate guardian.

Yet again, she wondered if she was the guinea pig, the test subject to see if she could handle it. If she couldn't fight them, they would use it on other gate guardians. If she could handle it, they'd go back to the drawing board.

At this rate, she'd never return to her body. Was that the whole point?

Being in two places at one time was exhausting for a body.

"Hey!" a gruff, angry voice boomed.

Omigod, the same maintenance man. Next, he'd call the police and then it would be on the local news.

Girl vanishes and reappears and... *another portal... no!*

Yep.

She vanished again! And she hoped the man wouldn't think he was losing his mind. Not that he had appeared that way. He looked more like he believed she was playing some Halloween-worthy trick on him. He wanted to know just how she was doing it. And he would put a stop to it.

This time she was in the reptile house. She didn't see a portal, nor a summoner. She didn't think a demon was here. At least not visible. Not that they could often hang around invisibly. Though Samson could. But she felt different.

Her skin chilled with awareness. Then her breath grew frosty, and she whipped about. Indigo was breathing down her neck.

"Where have you been?" Indigo asked. "I've been hopping all over thissss zzzzoo, looking for you. He'sss here."

She felt it, too. "Matusa," she whispered.

He nodded and pointed to a work room where they milked the snakes for venom to prepare anti-venom for snakebite victims.

"Where is the summoner?" she whispered, fearing whoever it was would probably be dead. She looked back at the room, eyes widening. What if the Matusa was using the poisonous bite of a snake on a hapless summoner? Several bites from poisonous snakes could do the job right and ensure that whoever summoned him would never do so again.

Heart skittering, she heard someone approaching the reptile exhibit and sirens nearing the entrance to the zoo. "Police are on their way. Wait, first units are already arriving. We're searching for the girl... or I should say the camera relaying the projection. No, I swear she was as real as you or me. And she answered me, just as if she was standing beside me. A projection can't do that. Nor how would she, or the projection, know how to answer me correctly? All right. I'm nearing the entrance of the reptile house. I'll check it out."

No, she wanted to scream. If the demon was in the reptile room and the maintenance man saw him, the Matusa would kill him without blinking an eye.

Before she could rush out of the reptile house to intercept the maintenance man, the door opened to the work room.

Matusa. Gorgeous. Why did something so evil have to appear so beautiful?

Dark lashes framed dark eyes. He was wearing a cap with a tiger on it, his long black hair curling about his shoulders. He gave her an almost imperceptible smile. "*Kubiteron*," he said in a seductive way that meant she was his for the taking. Only she wasn't. Not in this form. "Tell me, where are you?" He reached out to touch her, but realizing his mistake, he dropped his hand at his side. She might look real, but she was anything but.

"Who are you? What are you doing here?" she asked in a whisper.

"You know why I'm here. I've been summoned."

Yeah, she knew that part. But why was he here in this particular place, hiding in the reptile house? "And the summoner?" She hated to ask, but she suspected he was dead.

"He was some idiot who had designed a device to remotely summon portals ten at a time. Except that all it does is infuriates my kind."

Past tense. The summoner *was* some idiot. But he wasn't any longer.

Then the rest of the words the demon spoke sank in. *A device could remotely summon ten portals at a time.* Alana stared at the Matusa blankly. What a disaster that would be for those like her who were trying to stop the demons from being summoned to this world.

"Why would this infuriate you? More of you can slip into our world then, right?" Certainly, it would make it much more difficult for her to stop them.

"No." He looked angry, and she was afraid he'd turn his fury on her, but remembered that she was only an astral projection, and he couldn't hurt her. The form felt so real sometimes, it was getting to be difficult to remember that. "The portal collapsed in on itself and killed nine of my brethren before I was able to make it through this one. And take care of the summoner. One of us had to do it." He smiled, and the look was pure cold-blooded evil.

She could understand his need to stop the summoner from killing more Matusa. Some were just as reluctant to leave their world as were the lesser demons. None could help the call of a summoner. Only the Matusa could do something about it *after* they were summoned.

"I know what you are, Kubiteron. And I know *who* you are. *Alana Fainot.* You have visited our world and I was one of the ones who saw you there at the hall of records, and even participated in the battle between your witch's kind and my own people. I know the Matusa named Hunter who wants you for his own. Many are willing to risk taking you home and making you theirs. Partly because you are a Kubiteron and the choicest of mates. But also because you now serve in the position of guardian, and we would rather you live among us and no longer have the ability to thwart us here on Earth."

"Ha!" she said, forgetting the maintenance man, who was still talking on his phone. "You won't ever be able to take me from here to the demon's world."

The Matusa's mouth curved up just a hint. "The others may want you, but you will be mine. As soon as I discover where your physical being is, you and I will return to Seplichus. It's what you want, isn't it? For me to be gone from this world?" He held his finger up to his lips. "Company's coming. Remember me. I am Thorst."

"Don't you dare—," she began to warn the Matusa, not wanting him to kill the man. Though there wasn't anything she could do about it.

The Matusa stepped into the workroom and shut the door. It was up to Alana to cover for what he had done. Not cover for him, exactly, but keep him from killing the maintenance man also, should he find the dark-haired stranger in the work room with the dead body of the summoner.

Her mother would surely get a call from the police. She'd have to pick Alana up at school, too, until her astral and physical forms could rejoin. How long had it been?

Alana glanced at her watch. Holy cow! Two hours. Two class periods.

Poor Samson! He might have already alerted her mother. Or not. He really didn't trust her since she wasn't at least half demon.

Alana rushed outside, and the maintenance guy dropped his phone and swore up a storm. Before he picked up his phone, he grabbed for her. Maybe to satisfy his curiosity that she was just a projection. Maybe forgetting that she really wasn't there because she looked so real. Or maybe he thought she truly was the real girl this time.

What if after she was able to leave this place, *if she was able to leave this place*, they investigated the whole zoo, looking for the camera and found a dead man in the reptile room. And she'd been there, trying to stop the maintenance man from investigating it.

She'd kill the Matusa, Thorst, that got her involved in this mess.

She jumped back from the man before he connected, or rather, didn't connect, as he grabbed for her. To her astonishment, he managed to seize her arm. Her *solid* arm. And she did what any sane out-of-body person would do.

She shrieked.

CHAPTER 3

"Where is she?" Hunter asked Samson, not even letting him get a word in edgewise as he picked Hunter and Jared up at the airport and ushered them to her car in short-term parking.

"Well," Samson said, and the way he said *well* in an elongated fashion, Hunter knew he wasn't going to like this.

His heart had been charging hard on the whole plane trip, and he couldn't stop it from racing no matter how much he had told himself Alana would be all right. The thing of it was, she could very well be at death's door... and...

"Well, what?" Hunter asked, irritated, ready to slug the words out of Samson.

"She's in two places."

"All this time, still?" Hunter said incredulously.

Jared whistled in disbelief from the back seat of the

car.

"She couldn't be. Not unless a portal had remained open that long. She would have closed it. What's going on?" Hunter asked, his mind racing now as fast as his heart.

"Like I said," Samson started again, "she's in two places. She's at a hotel room, and she's at the police station."

"What?" Hunter wasn't getting it. If someone tried to take her astral self somewhere, they couldn't. She wasn't really physically there. Even if she tried to leave with the police officers without them touching her, she couldn't be a long way from a portal. She would just... vanish. Wouldn't she? At least that's what she used to do.

"We don't know. I swear she's still at the hotel, and her mother is with her at the police station. I don't think I've ever seen her mother so upset. It's like Alana is truly at the police station. But she can't be. I have the zombie version of her at the hotel."

"And you want to be her mate?" Jared asked.

Both Samson and Hunter gave Jared a quelling look.

"Sorry," Jared said.

"So her abilities have morphed again, and she can be in a solid form in two places," Hunter guessed.

"Remember her father said he could do that?" Jared asked helpfully.

"Yeah. So how does she get back to her real physical self?" Hunter asked.

"Probably have to get the two of them together. I didn't want to bring Alana to the airport in the event she's been seen on the news and passengers or employees wondered if she had escaped the police and was trying to flee the country."

"But if her mother is with her astral self, who's with her physical form? You know she shouldn't be left alone!" Hunter said, finally realizing she was alone.

"No, no, we have another demon watching over her."

Hunter stared at him. "Did you tell him to keep his hands off her?"

Samson had the guts to smile at him. "The demon is a girl."

Hunter relaxed a little, trying to calm his rapid breathing. His eyes had to be brilliant red by now. "Okay, you can tell me about her later. But back up a bit. What news? Why would Alana need to escape the police?" Hunter was getting a really bad feeling about this. Then realized he hadn't even asked why she was at the police station in the first place.

"A Matusa killed a summoner at the reptile house at the Baltimore zoo. That's where Alana was. At least, her astral self. Alana was a witness. Or so they say. So, now she's in custody. Or, at least one half of her is."

Hunter couldn't believe it. Then again where Alana was concerned... *he could.*

***

Alana might look real to all these people at the

police station, the two who were questioning her, and the myriads she believed were watching through the mirrored glass of the interrogation room, but keeping up her look-alike astral projection in full body form was taking a toll on her. She didn't think she could keep up appearances forever. She glanced at her mother sitting at the end of the table, looking at her as though she would do anything to get her out of this mess, short of killing anyone.

Her mother had already tried several times to convince the detectives interrogating Alana to let her go, and she wasn't making any headway. Not when the police highly suspected Alana had seen the killer. And they were worried for her safety.

If Alana had been in her physical form and could see the person eye-to-eye, she could have made each of them forget that she even existed. In her astral form, she couldn't do that witch's trick. Although she couldn't convince those watching from behind the mirror even if she was in her physical form, not without seeing them eye to eye.

"I don't know what the killer looked like," she repeated for the third time. *Gorgeous. To die for.* If the humans did back him into a corner, she had no doubt he'd take them all out. "I didn't see anyone in the reptile exhibit except reptiles."

"What kind of reptiles?" Detective Ryker asked, throwing her for a loop. Police detectives liked to do that sort of thing. Keep grilling the one under interrogation with details about a crime, then switching to something so different that it threw the perp off the track.

Just like it did her.

She had to guess. She didn't have any idea what was in the reptile exhibit this morning except she suspected lizards and snakes. So that's what she said. And hoped they really were in the exhibit or she was in even bigger trouble. Reptiles weren't her big draw to the zoo. Birds and mammals were.

Detective Ryker looked like a hard-charger, hair all chopped off like he was rough and tough and ready to get his man. Even if his man was a seventeen-year-old girl who couldn't kill a flea. Or at least looked that way. She probably had eliminated more bad guys in the form of ghosts and demons than he'd ever taken down, well, human variety, in his whole police career. And she was just getting started.

His eyes were hard gray shards of steel, and he didn't look like he had a sympathetic bone in his body. He was the one who would play hardball. She wondered if he had any kids. Woe to his kids if he did. They probably had to walk on the proverbial egg shells around him. No messing around. No getting into trouble. Or they'd be dead meat.

Detective Saunderson was the softy of the two. He looked totally sympathetic, as if he was on her side and was worried the bad guy might be out to get her if she could identify him. That she wasn't safe in the least. Well, she had news for the detective. He would be right.

When she found wherever her body was and reunited with it, she wouldn't be safe. Not from one highly interested and deadly serious Matusa demon.

"Mr. Bradshaw, the maintenance man at the zoo," Detective Ryker said, flipping through his notebook, "said you were talking to someone in the exhibit." He glanced at her again with that hard look that threatened her to fess up or else.

Her skin prickled with unease. Her hands sweated. A dribble of perspiration ran between her breasts. She was sure the room was ice cold, but she was growing hotter. The maintenance man must have had abnormally great hearing. She had whispered the words to the Matusa. She thought the Matusa had also. But maybe he had spoken out loud. She'd been so concerned about what he'd done and what he intended to do, she hadn't really been paying that much attention.

"What was the man's name?" Detective Saunderson asked.

Thorst, came to mind. "I didn't see anyone. I talked to no one. I just saw reptiles." *And a pesky ghost and a deadly demon.* The police detectives wouldn't believe her if she told them the truth.

Changing tack, Detective Ryker asked, "How did you project yourself from one place to another?"

"I didn't." They could look to kingdom come but they wouldn't find a projector anywhere. Mr. Maintenance Man had to have been mistaken.

The two detectives leaned back in their chairs. The

only good thing about any of this was that she had thoroughly confused them. Other officers would have been conducting a thorough background check on her and her mother, but they wouldn't find anything on her father. He didn't exist. Not unless they took a visit to the demon world, that none of them believed existed. Nothing indicated either she or her mother had been in any kind of trouble with regard to violating law enforcement issues.

In other words, neither had a rap sheet. As for Alana, she'd never been in trouble at school either. No skipping school. No bad grades. Nothing.

Detective Ryker flipped through his notebook again, and she was really beginning to dislike the man. She imagined he could make anybody feel guilty even if he or she hadn't done anything bad in their whole life. She was certain he'd dredge up some memory of something that wasn't exactly a proper way to behave in polite society and then the person being interrogated would feel as guilty as he was making him out to be.

He cleared his throat. "We checked into your school records. Talked to some of your teachers from last year."

She folded her arms and looked cross. Her school records were fine. Average to above average to excellent student, depending on the subject. No trouble with other students. She left them alone and they left her alone. Teachers had no trouble with her except...

She tried to stop the way her heart began racing again. She'd teleported a few times at the end of the school year, left her body, and heavens knew what the teachers thought. Well, that she was having coma-like symptoms that they couldn't understand. Trips to the school nurse ensued, and then Mom had to make up doctor's reports that said she was just having a slight seizure in class. They had a standing order: Call her mother and have her picked up at school if it happens again.

"You've had some medical trauma at school."

She didn't say anything. He was waiting for her to describe in detail how it all went down. She hadn't known what had happened. She hadn't been there. At least not mentally. That was one trick she couldn't do yet. Be fully in two places at the same time. How weird would that be? Trying to answer questions from different locations at the same time? Or trying to do two different actions at the same time in different places? Just plain unthinkable.

When she didn't enlighten him, he continued, "The record states you have seizures from time to time. What brings them on?"

Portals opening into the demon world. Summoners who try to bring demons here to make them work for them.

She shrugged.

"Trauma? Upset?"

She didn't respond. She must have looked like an annoyed teen, she imagined. At least that was the look she was trying to project.

"Did you have a seizure when you went into the reptile room? Is that why you couldn't remember the man who was there?"

The officer had done it again. Thrown her off track. She wasn't sure how to answer him without causing him to ask another barrage of questions.

Cautiously, she said, "Maybe I did have a seizure. If I did, I wouldn't have seen a man in the reptile exhibit. I wouldn't have seen anything. That's the way it works. I have no memory of what happens. Ever." She didn't fully lie. She didn't remember everything of the place when she left it on her astral trip, if she'd been having one of her out-of-body experiences. She might remember some details, but others she wouldn't. Like waking from a dream.

She didn't lie about not seeing a man, either. He was a demon. And she hadn't seen the summoner, who had probably been a man. Or possibly a warlock. A lone warlock was well out-matched by a deadly Matusa.

"Several students said you were in class, including a kid named Ferengees Samson, who said he walked you to your next class even." He paused and that pause was to make her think about Samson, to squirm in her seat, to make her wonder where the questioning was going.

She did think about Samson. About how he was managing. About what he'd done with her physical form.

But she wasn't going to squirm. She was really controlling her physical reaction, to an extent. She couldn't stop the way her heart was pounding against her ribs, or the way her hands were so dreadfully clammy. She was sitting so stiffly in the chair, she realized even that posture was a sign she was tense and worried. If she could, she should sag a little, untense her muscles, appear more relaxed. If she did that now, would she look defeated instead? Unable to hold up under the interrogation? Or even sassy? Indolent?

So, she remained stiff and felt that she'd made a mistake in the way she held herself, but there was nothing to do be done about it now. The pause in his speech did make her worry about where he was going with the questioning.

After a lengthy pause, Ryker continued, "The teacher worried that you were having a seizure."

Uh-oh.

"You were supposed to have gone to the nurse's station, but the nurse said you never arrived."

Each time, Ryker paused, waiting for a reaction, waiting to see if Alana knew very well what had happened to her while she'd been in the class.

"When the nurse checked, she found you were in class. Samson was to take you to the doctor and call your mother. But your mother was still at work. Samson took you in your car and left the school. Where did he go? Did he take you to the zoo? Why would he have taken you there if you were having one of your seizures? Did you fake having one?"

Ohmigod, Samson. They couldn't believe he had anything to do with the killing.

Detective Ryker tapped his pen on his notebook. She wanted to break the pen in two. "He's new to the school. Where's he from?" he asked.

A village in the demon world. And this was going to get really bad, really fast.

They wouldn't be able to find any record of him. He could very well be the man who had killed the other. If the detectives were trying to find a scapegoat, Samson was the perfect one for the job.

"You'll have to ask him."

Ryker gave her an accusatory glare. "We would, but we can't locate him."

He was hiding her real self, protecting her. Now he was in trouble because of her, and she felt awful because of it.

"How do you know him so well if he just moved here and today was your first day back to school?"

She had to tell the truth in part. Or else they'd know she was covering up for him for some reason. They'd most likely assume he killed the man, but she wouldn't let on. "We met at Holiday World."

Detective Ryker's brows rose marginally. "Holiday World. And how did that come about?"

He helped them to fight bad demons. Jeez, give her a break!

"We met at one of the rides."

"Which ride?"

Omigod, if Ryker got hold of Samson before she was able to, he'd grill him, too, and what would Samson say?

"I don't remember."

He looked over at her mother and said, "Do you remember what ride Samson and Alana met at, Mrs. Fainot?"

How could things get any worse? Her mother wasn't even there. She didn't even know that Alana had been there, either. As hot as Alana's face was, she was sure it was crimson.

"Why, I was working," her mother said, glancing at Alana, a concerned expression on her face. It wasn't so much as worrying about what she'd done, but more that she didn't know how to protect her. Alana loved her mother for it.

"You were working at Holiday World?" the detective asked her mother.

"No, here. In Baltimore."

"So you were with other family?" Detective Ryker asked Alana. "Your uncle out of Dallas, perhaps?"

This wasn't going to get any easier. She sighed. "I was with friends."

"Names?"

What a nightmare. Even her mother looked expectantly to see what she said.

"Hunter and Jared of Dallas."

"Last names?" She swore Detective Ryker was fighting a smirk. The good little girl who never caused any trouble was now in the midst of one big mess of it.

"I don't know their last names."

He straightened. "You went with two men to Holiday World when you didn't even know their last names? How old were they?"

They were demon hunters. And so was she. She saved their butts. They saved hers. Last names just didn't seem to be that big a deal. But the age thing... she was jail bait. And they'd been eighteen. Both of them. Or at least she knew Hunter was.

"Listen, they're friends. We helped each other when Hunter was really sick. He stayed with me and my uncle. My uncle can vouch for them."

That took Detective Ryker down a notch. She was certain he thought he had her over a barrel.

"Okay, I'll do that. So when you were at Holiday World, where did you all stay?"

She was back in the frying pan. "The Wonder Hotel."

"Separate rooms?" His pen was poised over his notebook, his head tilted down, but his eyes were looking up at her in an accusing manner.

At least she felt it was accusing. Particularly once he learned of the details. She felt hot all over again.

"Same hotel room. But the guys were gentlemen and stayed on the fold-out couch." *Only* because she'd forced the issue. The Matusa did not sleep on fold-out couches. At least according to Hunter.

"Hunter and Jared?"

She nodded.

"What about Samson?"

She couldn't tell him he'd stayed with them also. No way.

She glanced at her mother. Her eyes were huge.

Okay, so she hadn't told her mother all that had happened. But everything had been on the up and up. And she *had* slept in the bedroom. *Alone.*

If she said Samson had stayed at another hotel, they'd check it out and find she'd lied. If she told them Samson had stayed with them, the detectives would discover they hadn't paid for another occupant sleeping in the room. Unless Jared had made adjustments with the billing clerk. His parents paid for everything so she thought he might have done so.

"He stayed with us."

"On the fold-out sofa? Kind of crowded for three grown males, wasn't it?" Detective Ryker said.

"Samson slept on a roll-a-way bed."

"Hmm." Detective Ryker sneaked a glance at Alana's mother. She looked a bit pale.

Alana tilted her chin up higher. The one time she'd been in a hotel with three guys and not one of them had hit on her and it was all perfectly legitimate. They were demon fighters and watching each other's backs. If they hadn't stuck together, one or all of them might have been dead. Although she'd had to beat on Hunter, but that had been a necessary thing. She wasn't about to tell the detectives about that.

Or her mother.

"You never did say how old the men were."

Not sure. Which was the case in Samson's situation. She had no idea how old he really was. Hunter was eighteen for sure. She wasn't certain about Jared. Seventeen or eighteen.

As if he was truly worried that older men had taken advantage of her and they had a new case to try, Detective Saunderson broke in, "Twenty-five? Twenty? Ballpark figure?"

"My age," she said.

The detective nodded. "We don't believe you had anything to do with the killings, Alana," he said in a fatherly voice. He looked as though he wanted to reach out and pat her arm. She moved her hands under the table in her lap to keep them out of view.

Everything she did or said they could construe as guilt, she figured. She tried to look them straight in the eye, not fidget, appear as though she had nothing to hide. But she had everything to hide. It was becoming harder and harder to do. She was a half demon, half witch, gate guardian who astral traveled. All of which was pure fantasy as far as these men were concerned.

Her eyes were drooping with weariness, her heart rate slowing despite how nervous she felt. She couldn't maintain two bodies at the same time without something giving out.

Detective Ryker gave her a half smile that was faked to high heaven. She knew just how to offer one of those when she didn't mean it in the least. "We think you went to the zoo to see the lions like you told the maintenance man."

Liar. He didn't think anything like that at all. He was trying to get her to spill the truth, and then they'd hang her with it.

"You probably saw the man enter the reptile house, and you wondered what he was up to."

"Can I go now?" Alana asked, and was surprised to hear how tired her voice sounded.

Her mother looked even more worried than before, if that was possible.

"Just a few more questions," Detective Ryker said with authority.

She could tell he loved his job. She knew he'd ask the same questions over again, take more notes, keep recording all she said. As soon as she slipped up just once, he'd have a field day. Begin the questioning all over again. Grind her down until he proved she knew who the man was, that she'd lied about speaking to him, that she'd been in cahoots with him even.

"How did you get from the school to the zoo without your car? No one saw you arrive at the front gates, the ticket booth, anywhere. When the maintenance man reported you were on the premises, security checked for your vehicle. No unaccounted vehicles were in the lot. No busses came to the area, either."

"I walked."

"Not from the school. The times just aren't matching up, though, anyway we see it. Everyone says you were in classes, but they can't be right. You don't have a twin, do you?" He glanced at Alana's mother as if she'd have a better answer.

"No. Alana's an only child."

Detective Ryker focused on Alana again. "So how did you get there? Did you start walking, then this man picked you up and you wandered around the animal exhibits before Mr. Bradshaw caught sight of you?"

A tingling throughout her body warned Alana another portal had opened. She couldn't astral travel out of the interrogation room without sending everyone, including her mother, into a state of hysteria.

"I need to go to the bathroom."

"In a minute. Now about..."

Alana stood up. "*Now*. I need to go *now*." Like immediately!

CHAPTER 4

The two police detectives stared at Alana as if she'd asked for a paid trip to the moon.

"I have to go to the bathroom *now*," she insisted, not waiting for them to allow it as she walked to the door of the interrogation room.

"All right. A police woman will go with you," Detective Ryker said, as if warning her she wasn't going to escape. But she was.

She imagined someone watching through the mirrors had already contacted a policewoman in a hurry.

She cast her mother a sympathetic look, mouthed, "I love you," then as soon as the door to the room opened, she hurried into the hall saying, "Which way? Which way?"

She was as desperate as she felt, and the policewoman who had rushed to escort her looked hard at her as if she figured Alana was faking she had to go to the bathroom. Her expression changed to concern as desperate as Alana truly had to look.

And she was desperate, feeling as though she was being torn from the place by the strength of a hurricane as she struggled to remain here.

As soon as she was in the restroom's stall, the woman asked, "Are you sick, honey?"

Alana couldn't respond while she was on her way out of there. She hated to think what would happen to the poor lady. She would relate how Alana had just vanished in thin air, just like the maintenance man had most likely said she had done at the zoo.

Her poor mother would probably be questioned for hours. Alana couldn't help it. She just couldn't have vanished in front of the mirror and the two detectives.

The next thing Alana knew, she was standing before a blue and green light filled portal, the wind whipping about her inside a small hotel room and other than the lights, she noticed the cheerful yellow walls, red carpet, and sunflowers against red skies in pictures on the wall behind the portal.

She stared into the light, mesmerized. She knew that demons came through the portals. That summoners tried to force the demon to do their bidding, and she needed to know what threat existed in the room. Yet she was so drained from energy, all she could do was stare at the lights.

Jared said, "She's here, Hunter! I told you when all else fails you can make her come to you by opening a portal."

She whipped around, not believing Hunter and Jared were truly here, although Jared's comment thoroughly irritated her. Hunter did *not* control her through summoning portals. At least, he better not think he could.

She saw Samson smiling at her, and her own self lying on a queen-sized bed next to another, both covered with spreads that were red, decorated with huge yellow daisies. Her eyes were closed. Her heart began skipping beats, and she felt dizzy.

"Alana." Hunter rushed forth to grab her, but she vanished in his arms.

Everyone was staring at Hunter as if he'd lost Alana again, and she would have smiled as she reclined on the mattress, if she hadn't been so tired.

"Here," she said weakly. "Close the portal, will you?"

Hunter did so, then turned and rushed to the bed and took her ice-cold hands in his. "What the hell happened?"

"I'm in really big trouble."

His expression was smug amusement and all-knowing, like he could have told her that's what she always was.

That's when she noticed the disquieting blonde from calculus class, sitting on the other bed. "Who is she?"

"Celeste Sweetwater," the girl said with a small smile.

Alana frowned at her and said to Hunter, "What is

she doing here?" Telepathically she said, *"She can't learn what we are."*

Hunter couldn't telepathically speak with Alana, but he could hear her and so he said, "She's one of us."

Alana should have been thrilled to have a girlfriend among her friends. But she wasn't. What was wrong with her? Jealous that she'd been the center of attention all this time, and now she'd have to share the spotlight with a girl who looked older and sexier?

Yeah, that was it. Sexier. And older.

"She's not a demon," Alana said to him alone. *"I don't see any demon aura around her."*

"She's a demon," Hunter said.

"What kind? Are you cloaking your demon aura or does your kind just not reveal itself in the form of an aura?" Alana asked Celeste.

"Camaron."

"You can cloak yourself?" Alana asked, then yawned. She couldn't help it. She needed to sleep... desperately.

"Full Camaron. And yes, I can cloak my demon aura."

Alana instantly felt sorry for the girl. She had to have been pulled from her world against her will. "What... are you doing here? Were you summoned?"

"Oh yes."

"What are you doing *here* then? Where's your summoner? Is he or she letting you go to school?"

"They were killed by a Matusa years ago. I was...

too young to be on my own. So I ended up in foster homes. I moved here from Oklahoma and just started my senior year of high school. Then I saw Samson in calculus class, and you." She smiled. "I thought we might be friends."

Rather she had her sights set on Samson. Alana smiled back, glad the girl wasn't interested in Hunter. But then she frowned. "We can send you back. Both Hunter and me. We can open a portal and return you to your world."

"No way. Chance getting called back to Earth by some human summoner? I was three when I was pulled here. I have no idea who my real parents were, and I have no memories of living in the demon world. I'll take my chances here. So what's the trouble you've gotten yourself into?"

"You probably know I astral travel."

Celeste nodded. "The guys filled me in that you were a gate guardian."

"Yeah, and I happened to run across a Matusa who killed his summoner at the zoo in the reptile house."

Hunter frowned at Alana, then looked at Jared. "Tracking any?"

Jared was looking at a small handheld device. He shook his head.

"Is that the new Demon Tracker II?" Alana asked, her interest piquing.

"Yeah."

"Is it working?"

"Like a charm."

She scowled. "Good, then you can hand it right over. I'll know when this guy is after me then."

Jared snorted. "Hunter said we didn't need them. Just you because you're like a Matusa demon magnet. Or words to that effect."

She gave Hunter a dirty look. He squeezed her hand and cast her a smidgeon of a smile. "It's true, isn't it? So what's the deal with this Matusa?"

For a moment, she couldn't think of anything, but the way Hunter was holding her hand as if he was afraid to let go of her. Grasshoppers hopped around in her belly as she stared up at him. "Alana," he said quietly, and she saw the worried look in his dark gaze.

She cleared her throat. "He said the summoner was building a device that would open ten portals at a time."

Hunter swore under his breath and was all business at once. "Where is it?"

"How would I know? I was pulled to the portals, never even saw them, the summoner, or a demon. The demon said that the portals collapsed inward and killed the other Matusa. He was the only one who got through. Thorst was his name."

"He told you his *name*?" Hunter frowned at her as if it was her fault the demon liked her.

She scowled right back at him. "*Of course,* he told me his name. He already *knew* mine."

Hunter's face darkened. "How?"

"Well, *I* didn't tell him!" She pulled her hand free

from his and folded her arms, looking crossly at him. "He saw me at the hall of records, and he saw us fighting… or I should say he was one of the ones fighting my uncle and his warlock companions while we helped them."

Hunter cursed again. "Great. The Matusa must have been watching for the portals to open then."

"I imagine so. They had to have been in the same area. So they probably gathered together, figuring they would come through all at about the same time and take care of a bunch of summoners. Only they didn't make it, and the summoner was just one man."

"We've got to destroy the device. We can't allow anyone else to get hold of it and summon lesser demons who could be killed in the process."

"I have to sleep, Hunter," Alana said, hating that she felt so wiped out and couldn't help them hunt the Matusa and the device right away.

"The rest of us can go," Celeste said.

At once, Alana felt resentful. She was glad that Celeste wanted to be on their team as they certainly could use more help, but she was new at the game, and no way did Alana want to be left out. For one thing, she was in the middle of this whole mess.

"We have to go, Hunter. We've got to locate the device now," Jared said, motioning to Alana. "You know. Before she gets herself into any more trouble." He gave her half a grin.

As much as Jared irritated her with his comment, she knew Jared was right. That Hunter was, too. And even

Celeste. Samson remained quiet.

If someone else controlled the portals and he opened them again, Alana would be sucked right into her astral form and dragged to the new portal.

She couldn't stop Hunter and the others from doing what was the sensible thing to do. She waved her hand at the air in such a tired motion, she could barely lift it. "Go. I'll sleep, and you can tell me what happened."

"You can't be left alone," Hunter said, looking worried again, although his voice was more commanding as if he was ordering her about rather than concerned about her.

She knew better. Yet she knew also that he'd want to lead the team. That was a Matusa way. He would assign someone to stay behind to watch over her. Jared, probably.

"Why not leave me alone? No one knows I'm here. Right? You might as well go as a team and get this done. The more of you there are, the safer it will be."

"I'm staying," Samson said, arms folded across his broad chest, looking determined.

Celeste looked like she wanted to object. Alana was all for Celeste and Samson getting together and maybe he could see how much she was interested in him. But then Alana thought better of it.

"Yes, Samson, you've got to stay."

Now Hunter looked even more worried, and she assumed he thought maybe while he'd been away, she'd developed an attachment to the Samuria.

She quickly added, "He's been implicated in the killing."

Hunter frowned at her.

Samson narrowed his eyes. "How?"

"Everyone knew you drove me from the school, but not where to. I ended up at the zoo where a man was murdered. I wouldn't tell them who the man was. You're new to the school. No one knows where you're really from. I had to tell them we met at Holiday World, no real history between us. So, you're the mystery man who was linked to the murder through no fault of your own. Sorry, Samson. I couldn't think of any way to un-implicate you."

Samson ran his hands over his hair. "Great. Then it's decided. I stay with you." At that, he gave her a small smile, like it pleased him no end.

Hunter looked like he wanted to object. But reconsidered. If Samson was seen and picked up, all of them could be considered accessories to some crime that none of them had committed. At least not yet. As soon as they got hold of the Matusa, he'd be dead.

"What about the Matusa?" Hunter asked.

"Oh, the usual," Alana said. "He wanted me. Vowed to find me and take me home with him. Use me for his own wicked purposes." She smiled. "But you know how I feel about offers like that."

Hunter was looking so darkly at her, she frowned back. "What? You know I would have kicked some demon butt if I could have. I was in my astral form. He couldn't grab me, and I couldn't do him any bodily harm either. Or at least at the time we both thought he couldn't grab me. The maintenance man proved otherwise."

Jared said, "He sounds like he might be the same one who called you, Hunter."

Alana's mouth gaped. "Did I miss something?"

"He said you were his and hung up on me. Why call me and warn me? Why not just grab you?"

"Probably because he saw you fighting before the hall of records. Is that why you're here?" The fog still surrounded Alana's brain but then for a minute, she had some clarity. "Why *are* you here?"

"We got the call from a Matusa, and then Samson gave us a ring while we were on the way to the airport."

"Thanks, Samson," Alana said.

His chest puffed up. "Your astral form hadn't returned to your body. I wasn't sure what to do."

Hunter looked exasperated that she'd thank Samson and not him and Jared. They'd flown all morning to get here. All Samson did was stand around a hotel room. Or at least that's all he had better have been doing, Alana thought.

"Why would he call you?" Alana finally asked Hunter. She guessed her thought processes weren't all that clear.

"That's what I wondered."

"Revenge," she said. "Maybe someone you pissed off in the demon world, and he wants revenge."

"Could be. You ready to go?" Hunter asked Jared.

"Yeah. Got our devices and…"

"Leave one with me," Alana said.

"No doing," Hunter said. "You're in no shape to join us. Stay put. Besides, you're probably just as wanted by the police as Samson."

She snorted, folded her arms, and closed her eyes. "Fine. Go. Get the bad guys. I already had my turn today." Although she hadn't accomplished anything but getting herself and Samson in trouble.

She felt lips pressed against her mouth, and she opened her eyes. Hunter smiled down at her. "Sweet dreams, Alana."

She grabbed his hand and squeezed, her eyes filling with a shimmer of unwanted tears. "Don't get yourself killed. Again."

His smile broadened. "If I do, you can beat me back to life. We'll be back shortly."

Then he and Jared and Celeste were out the door. "We'll move Alana's car from here first and find someplace to hide it," Hunter ordered. "We'll take Celeste's car on the hunt.

Then, they were gone. But not the feeling that more trouble was just about to begin.

CHAPTER 5

Celeste drove Hunter and Jared to the zoo, still shocked to learn that more of her kind were living on Earth world. She wasn't sure how to feel exactly. Gratified she might finally fit in, or mortified that she would be caught up in a world of danger, much more than she'd had to deal with in the past.

She shouldn't have been so surprised. If she'd been brought through a portal, why not others?

"He killed the summoner," Celeste finally said, casting a glance at Hunter. She was used to telling her foster parents about her visions. Well, not anything demon related. *That,* she'd kept a secret. But she still felt uncomfortable telling Hunter or Jared or any of the others a whole lot about herself.

What if they didn't like Camaran demons? She had no idea what experiences they'd had with others of her kind. What if they didn't like what she was able to do?

She still couldn't believe Hunter was a Matusa, even though he was only half, but was still one of the good guys.

"That's what Alana said," Hunter concurred, but he gave her a concerned look, like he suspected she was going to reveal something further.

He'd accepted her readily into their little group of demon hunters once she'd un-camouflaged her aura. Jared was different. He didn't like it that she was joining them. He didn't say so, but his scowl told her another story.

"Yes, that's what Alana said," Celeste agreed. "But she didn't see the Matusa kill the summoner. Not actually. She only guessed he had. Then learned from the police that he had."

"You... weren't... there," Hunter said slowly, but he sounded like he realized she might have been, but he couldn't believe it.

She glanced in the rear-view mirror and noticed Jared staring at her, waiting for her to respond.

"Were you?" Hunter asked, when she didn't say.

"Sort of." She pressed her spine against the seat back, trying to ease the tension.

"What do you mean *sort of?*"

"I... envisioned it."

Jared swore under his breath and began tapping at the keyboard on his laptop.

"I saw a Matusa holding a snake's head, pressing exposed fangs into a human's juggler. The man was already paralyzed, his eyes wide, but he wasn't fighting the demon. Once I learned the murder took place at the reptile exhibit, I assumed he was the same Matusa that I had seen. *Envisioned,* rather."

"Psychic," Jared said from the back seat of the car. "It says here in my reference guide to demons that the Camaran are known to see future events." He sounded vehemently opposed to the notion, and she imagined he knew the rest.

He closed his laptop. "And they try to mess with the future so those events don't occur. Unless of course they want them to. And then they don't interfere."

"Can you?" Hunter asked. "Alter future events?"

"No." Celeste didn't want him or any of the others believing she could stop an event she envisioned from happening. Sometimes she could. Sometimes she couldn't. Maybe as she got older and became more experienced with it, she could control it more.

"You were at the zoo?" Hunter asked again.

"Yes." She parked the vehicle and motioned to a fence. "Over there." She chewed on her lower lip as she stared in the direction of the fence. She knew they had to do this, but what if the police were about? Or other employees? What if they got caught? "He cut through the chain link. The summoner."

"You were here at the same time that Alana was?" Hunter asked incredulously.

"No. I was here last night. I... envisioned the Matusa killing the summoner last night, but it didn't happen until I was in classes with Samson and Alana had astral shifted to the zoo."

"Why were you at the zoo last night?" Hunter asked.

"To change the outcome of future events," Jared said, answering for her. "What a mess that would have been. The summoner would have continued to kill demons by summoning them through several faulty duplicate portals."

"The Matusa could have been dead," Celeste said quietly. Except she'd realized as soon as she'd heard the demon die inside the portal last night something was horribly wrong, and she had to refigure her plan to go after the summoner. She'd never expected that he was operating several of them at once or that they would kill the summoned demons.

Then she'd unexpectedly found Alana, a gate guardian, who was drawn to the opening of a portal in an out-of-body sort of way. When she'd seen her sitting in class like a zombie, unresponsive to the teacher's questions and Samson looking worried to death over Alana, she'd uncamouflaged her own demon aura to let him know she was one of them. And offered to help him in any way that she could.

She hadn't planned to speak with him until she was certain he was one of the good guys, but anyone who was as studious as he was couldn't be all bad.

"I don't know that we'll find anything here that will clue us in as to who the summoner was or where he might have his portal duplicator machine. Or any lead as to where the Matusa went," she warned.

"We start at the beginning. If we don't find anything here, we'll go to the morgue and see if we can get the summoner's effects," Hunter said. "How did you know that you were a Camaran demon? If you were brought here when you were three, your summoners wouldn't have known. And we can't see our own aura."

"The Matusa who killed them told me. He looked straight at me and said, 'Camaran!'"

"And he didn't take you with him?" Jared asked.

"A three-year-old? Are you kidding?" Celeste snapped.

Hunter smiled darkly.

"What else does that list of yours say about my type?" Celeste asked.

"They can conceal their aura," Jared said.

They got out of the car and headed for the break in the fence.

"Anything else?" Hunter whispered to Jared.

"Yeah. Like Alana is drawn to portals, Camaran demons are drawn to danger. They like dangerous sports, fighting in wars, or police type work. So I'd say we have another demon on our hands who's bound to cause us more trouble."

"I'm not the enemy here," Celeste said, slipping in through the cut in the fence. She turned to Jared as he followed her inside the zoo. "Make me one of those demon detectors, too. Will you?"

"Hey, this requires a highly technical process. It's

not factory mass produced, you know. Right now, I'm working on one for Hunter and then one for me. And that's it."

Hunter gave him a dark look.

Jared scowled back at him. "And Alana. But that's it!"

"You know, I could have a future vision that shows you're in some kind of danger, and I could alter the future, so you would survive, if I had enough of an incentive," Celeste said.

Jared snorted. "You said you couldn't alter the future."

Celeste smiled in an evil way. "I lied. Put that in your list of attributes for a Camaran demon, Elantus," she said. Then she turned to Hunter. "Have you known Alana long?"

"For only the summer," Jared answered for him. "But it seems like forever."

Hunter glowered at him.

Celeste smiled. She had not had a brother. Even a human foster brother, but she loved seeing the interaction between Hunter and Jared. She could tell in the brief time she'd observed them, Hunter really did care about Jared. And Jared was loyal through and through to the Matusa. It seemed like a strange kind of friendship—a warrior teaming up with an electronic wizard. She realized then, each of the hunters had special skills. Each demon would, but the combination of the group would surely make it more difficult for the bad guys to win.

She thought Samson was more of a loner like she was, which was another reason she was attracted to him. She had wanted to see what he was capable of had he come with them. But since he'd been seen with Alana, she could understand how he might be wanted for questioning and put the rest of them at risk.

"You like Alana, even though you try to rile her," Celeste said to Jared. "Why?"

"She's a witch," he said, quite sincerely.

"She seems really nice to me."

Jared grunted. "She's really a witch. Like in—magic and spells kind of witch."

Celeste looked at Hunter to see if he agreed. He gave her a stiff nod.

"Which makes her unlike any Kubiteron there is," Jared said.

"Ah. So you can't analyze her by using your database on demon types," Celeste said.

"Yeah, she's totally unpredictable, like a wildcard."

They grew quiet as they made their way across the zoo as quickly as they could in the direction of the reptile house. They soon saw police scouring the area for evidence at the crime scene and the three of them stealthily made their way back to the fence.

"We'll go to the morgue and see if we can locate the summoner's effects," Hunter said.

"We need Alana," Jared said, which surprised Celeste because he seemed to put her down more than he was kind to her. Which made her wonder if he was interested in her when Hunter was definitely intrigued with the Kubiteron.

"With her ability to force people to do what she wants and wipe their minds that she's even been there, we really could use her," Jared said.

Celeste could tell Hunter did want to take Jared up on his suggestion, but then he said, "I'm certain that after she vanished from the police station, she'll be wanted for even more questioning."

"True," Jared said. "I'd say once we locate the portal device and destroy it, we'll need to take her somewhere else."

"We may have to," Hunter agreed, though he didn't sound like his heart was in it.

"Did Alana really save your life?" Celeste asked Hunter as they climbed back into the car and drove off.

"Three times," Jared said.

She cast a look at him over the back seat. He grinned at her and shrugged. "He doesn't mention the first time, only the other two times when she beat on him."

Neither explained what they meant, and she didn't ask, although she would query Alana when she had the chance. "Have you ever wished you were human?" she asked Jared, figuring that since Hunter was half human, he didn't need to answer.

Jared snorted. "And have all these human emotions?"

"Demons are just as emotional, though perhaps not

quite in the same way," she told him.

"Do you wish you were human?" Jared asked, his voice riddled with disbelief.

She thought about it as Jared directed her with the GPS as to how to proceed the quickest way to the hospital.

"No. At least I don't believe so. I think I'd have to be human and alternately demon to know which I would prefer for certain."

"Have you ever wanted to find your parents? To learn if you have siblings?" Jared asked.

"Do you?"

"Yeah, I do. I want them to know that I'm alive and well. Not so much that I want to live in the demon world since I've always lived *here*. But I'd like to know them. My human parents have been extremely generous with me, but I still would like to know where I come from."

"Speculating and knowing can be two very different stories," Hunter warned as they pulled into the parking lot of the hospital.

Jared didn't say anything for a minute, then as they left the car, he said, "I still want to know—good or bad."

Celeste realized then that Hunter might be afraid Jared would find something to shatter his illusion of what his parents would be like. Or maybe he was even afraid he'd lose Jared. That Jared would want to return home and stay in the demon world with his real family.

"I don't think I want to find mine," she said. "I would be afraid that they'd want me to stay in their world. I might not have a family I care for here like you do, Jared, but I still wouldn't want to return to the demon world."

"You don't even know anything about it from what you said."

"True." She took a deep breath and walked into the frigid hospital with Jared and Hunter. "But I've moved a lot over the years with foster parents, and I don't like it. I don't care for having to adjust to each new place, every new school, trying to make new friends. A world that's even more unreal to me would be even worse."

Hunter looked over at her. "We're going to have to move Alana, most likely. And Samson, when the police can't find anyone else to blame for the summoner's murder. Leave it to a Dark One to murder a human and ditch the body for others to have to explain. In fact, he may have done so to implicate Alana anyway, thinking she might have to take refuge in the demon world. Then he'd have her."

"He can't go back to his world without a human's help," Celeste said.

"True, he can't open a portal and send himself back. He could force a human to do it."

She let out her breath. So they would have to move Alana and Samson. Was he hinting that she could go with them also? He didn't come out and say she could go with them. Maybe he didn't want to because she was living with foster parents. Maybe he was afraid if she disappeared, it would cause more trouble for the rest of them. If Samson and Alana disappeared from the same class and so did Celeste, some might believe she was with them. She assumed, being that he was a Matusa, he would be the one who would decide to ask her if she wanted to go with them or not.

Would she want to? It seemed to her that if she did, she'd end up in a skillet of burning oil faster than anything. The quirky demon side of her, which since she was all demon, meant the whole of her being, was fascinated with the idea. Yet, they were higher ranked demons—both the Matusa and the Kubiteron. She didn't know where her type fit in the ranking of powerful demons. She didn't think her abilities were all that powerful. At least not yet.

So far, all she could do was see glimpses of the future and sometimes stop events from happening. Which meant if she returned to the demon world, she could be at the bottom of the totem pole and that didn't agree with her at all.

When they reached the morgue, Hunter took charge. Celeste knew he would.

But nothing went right from the beginning. She and Jared stayed outside the room, but when Hunter went in, he was only there for a second and back out again. "Police," he whispered.

"What did you say?" she asked.

They all hurried for the door.

"I was told my Uncle Andrew was here and I had to ID him, but I had the wrong place."

Jared said, "Okay, so now what do we do?"

"We return to the hotel and wait until it gets late. We'll check the morgue for the guy's effects then." Hunter turned to Celeste and said, "What did you do about leaving school early?"

"I just left. I followed Alana's car until Samson parked at the hotel, and then hailed him."

"He didn't even know someone was tailing him?" Hunter sounded as though he was ready to strangle him. "He's her bodyguard, or so he claims! What kind of a bodyguard would let a stalker sneak up on him."

"He knew I was behind him. He pulled the car over, and I parked behind him." Celeste turned to Jared. "How do we get to the hotel from here?"

He gave her directions and they got in her car and drove off. "Stop for carryout first, would you?" Jason said.

"I don't have any money," Celeste warned.

"I do," Jared said.

"So, Samson pulled over and you parked behind him and...?" Hunter said to Celeste.

"He confronted me, and then he saw I was from their class and that I was a demon and I asked if I could help. I didn't know about the astral business. Just thought Alana was having some kind of demon seizure. Anyway, because we left the school in different vehicles, no one suspected I was with them."

"But you skipped school and when your foster parents learn of it, then what?" Hunter asked.

"I'll deal with it."

"You'll have to," Hunter said. "Jared and I have graduated from high school. His parents and mine know we're on our own, working, or so they think. Alana's mother is a witch, and her father is a demon. Both know her situation. Samson is probably older than all of us, and he's on his own. But you're living with foster parents who are clueless about what you are. And you still have another year of high school. So you have to go to classes just like any other regular human."

"Burgers? Chicken to go?" she asked, wanting to ignore Hunter. Here was the first time she felt a real sense of purpose, other than chasing after future visions and trying to right wrongs all on her own. Even though she barely knew any of these people, they were more like her than not.

They understand how different she was from others. She wanted to help them and wanted them to help her also. What was wrong in that?

On the other hand, she knew Hunter was right. If he and the others had to take Alana and Samson far away from here, she knew she couldn't go with them. She'd be a missing person. Her foster parents definitely wouldn't allow her to run off with three guys and another girl to who knew where.

She might have wanted to do so, but she couldn't cause more trouble for them also.

"My foster parents don't get home until late. They have a drinking party they're going to after work. I'll tell them I got sick at school, and my foster mother will write a note for me. Tomorrow, I'll go to school and if you'll give me your cell number, I can let you know what I hear around school."

Hunter nodded. She thought he even looked glum that he couldn't let her go with them. Jared didn't say a word. She wondered what he was thinking.

So much for finding her demon kick-butt team. She was on her own.

"Skip the burgers," Jared suddenly said. "A Matusa demon is headed in the direction of the hotel where Alana is staying."

CHAPTER 6

News about rising floodwaters in another state blared on the television in the hotel room first, then an annoying woman who was sobbing about her boyfriend being unfaithful on a soap opera-type story filled the airwaves, followed by an ad for wipes that would clean up any spill, and then a sports commentator giving a play by play.

Grinding her teeth and frowning, Alana tossed and turned, trying to sleep, to shake off her tiredness from astral traveling. She pulled the spare pillow over her head, but she couldn't block out all the noise. She finally yanked the pillow aside and glowered at Samson as he sat in a chair beside a table, eyes focused on the television, thumb poised on the channel changer. *"Quit... switching... channels!"* she demanded.

He raised his brows as he eyed her as if trying to figure out if she was serious or not.

"I'm… not… joking!" she said, her body still tired from being separated during the astral travel for longer than she'd ever done before. She hoped Hunter and the others were all right as they returned to the zoo to locate the portal creator device, but she was ready to kill one Samuria. Next time, she'd insist Jared stay with her instead. He could be annoying, but even so, she didn't think he'd be *this* annoying. "Either leave the T.V. on one channel, or turn it off."

"I could lie down," he said, smiling in a purely demonic way, motioning to the other side of the mattress.

"Your funeral if Hunter catches you in bed with me," she said, smiling just as evilly back. Then she scowled again. "But it's going to be your funeral anyway if you flip that channel one more time."

He held the channel changer in his hand, and the look on his face said it all. He was trying to decide whether to obey her or not.

"You know, you're supposed to listen to me, Samuria."

"Protect you," he corrected.

She snorted. "Who's going to protect you if you change the channel one more time?"

He chuckled, turned off the television, and sat down on the mattress next to her. "I'm not interested in her, Kubiteron," he said. "I'm here to serve you."

She let out her breath. "Fine. Serve me." She motioned to the chair that he'd been sitting on. "Stay there and protect me." She still had every intention of getting Samson together with Celeste. He had it in mind it was his duty to protect Alana and be her mate. There had to be more to a relationship than that.

She closed her eyes and sighed.

Samson's cell phone rang, and her eyes popped open. He immediately rose from the bed, jerked his phone out, and looked at the ID. "Hunter," he said.

She wanted to ask for the phone, but it was Samson's, and she was supposed to be resting. So, despite her wanting to be in charge of the situation and know immediately what Hunter and the others had found, she waited, impatiently.

Until Samson swore. "Right away." He shoved the phone in his pocket, yanked his keys out of his other pocket, then pulled Alana from the bed.

"Hey," she said in protest.

"Matusa is nearby."

She gritted her teeth. "I'm going to kill Jared. If he'd left one of his demon tracker devices with us, we would have known it before it was nearly too late."

"Wait."

It was already too late, she feared.

Samson shifted into a mist and slipped under the door. Not good. So not good.

A knock at the door sounded almost immediately after that. She stood frozen, staring at the door. Then something jiggled in the keyhole. If it was a key, it had to be Hunter with the others, right? Wishful thinking. If it had been Hunter, Samson would have sifted back into the room.

She hurried into the bathroom, looking for an escape route. No windows in there. No other windows in the hotel room except the ones facing the parking lot right next to the door. The *key* wasn't opening the door as quickly as it should if it was really the key for the room.

A thump followed and a string of curses. It wasn't Hunter, or Samson, or Jared. Someone else. Male, gruff, angry.

She wanted to help Samson, never having felt so unsure of herself before. Another thump. A grunt. Another slew of profanity. Then quiet.

Forever, she waited for a response. Nothing. She told herself to head for the door. To open it. To see what had happened. Fear took hold. If Samson wasn't returning, what would she do outside the room? Fight a Matusa? Alone. And if he was no longer there? She couldn't go anywhere anyway. Standing in front of the hotel was bound to get her into more trouble.

Then she heard the key again. *Samson.* What had happened to Samson? She didn't care if he thought he was her protector. She had every notion of being one of the team and that meant being there with them to help during a fight.

The door clicked. Unlocked.

Samson would have sifted back into the room as mist rather than suddenly appearing in front of her room in human form, risking that someone might see him. Wouldn't he have?

The door opened. She braced herself, ready to cast a spell. Hunter filled the doorway and rushed in, and stopped to see her standing there, hands up, ready to blast him with a water spell, if he'd been a fire demon. Her heart began beating again.

"Hunter," she said with relief, then hurried toward him. "Where's Samson?"

"He's supposed to be protecting you," he said gruffly and took hold of her hand.

"He was. He went outside and... I believe he was fighting the Matusa," she said, defending Samson for having left her.

Hunter squeezed her hand, but none of the strain in his expression eased as he pulled her out of the hotel room where Jared and Celeste waited just outside. "We have to get you out of here."

"But Samson..."

"He'll find us. It's his job to protect you. He knows you can't stay here."

"Uh, you want me to go home, right?" Celeste said, as she climbed into the driver's seat. "But... if I leave you off at Alana's car where you've hidden it, the cops will be looking for it and her, won't they?"

"Yeah. Take us to the airport," Hunter said. "We'll get a rental car there."

"You're not coming with us, Celeste?" Alana asked. She could see the disappointment etched in Celeste's expression, and she really did belong with them, Alana thought.

"She can't," Hunter said, moving Alana to the back seat of Celeste's car, then he slid in beside her.

"You let her drive?" Alana asked, shocked.

Hunter scooted closer to Alana and smiled. "Why not? It's her car."

"Yeah, but you never let me drive even when it's *my* car." Not that she really cared much who was driving, except it was Hunter's so controlling I'm-in-charge attitude that got to her at times. "So why does Celeste have to go?"

"She has to return to school. Your mother can say she's homeschooling you. Celeste needs to return home to her parents."

"*Foster parents*," Celeste said crisply.

"Or they'll think she's a missing teen. We can't afford to have her with us," Hunter said. "We've already got enough trouble."

Alana didn't like the idea. Celeste should be with them. She was one of them. In the future, Celeste was bound to get herself into trouble if she was on her own. "Even if I homeschool, it won't work. The police will be after me for disappearing at the police station," Alana reminded Hunter.

"Yeah, which means we'll have to let your mother know we're taking you somewhere else."

"I will." Alana leaned against Hunter and he wrapped his arms around her in a warm embrace. This was why she really had missed him, she had to admit to herself. His gruffness, his pretense that she couldn't live without him, when he truly cared for her, too, his tenderness at times like this.

"Are you still tired?" he asked.

"Yeah." She wasn't about to tell him that Samson's watching T.V. had deterred her from sleeping. Hunter was already irritated enough about the Samuria's interest in her so anything Samson did that annoyed her, exacerbated the situation between them. "I was in my astral form for three and a half hours because of the police interrogation. I'm not sure what happened. It's like once I was there, even if the portal was closed, I couldn't return to my physical form. When you opened the other portal, I was drawn back and was able to finally join my astral self with my physical one."

Jared cleared his throat.

Hunter said, "What, Jared?"

"Maybe now that we've got Alana with us and she can use her witchy powers, we could drop by the hospital morgue. She can do her spooky thing with controlling minds and have them turn over the summoner's personal effects."

Hunter looked at Alana to see her take on it.

"Sure. If it will help locate the summoner's portal devices, it sounds good to me."

"All right. We'll go there first," Hunter agreed.

Celeste detoured to the hospital.

Alana spoke with her mother telepathically to let her know what was going on, avoiding using the phone in the event the police were monitoring them.

"Mom, are you okay?"

"I'm home. Where are you?" Definitely her mother sounded on edge. Alana couldn't blame her. After Alana began having demonic powers, her mother had to acknowledge that Alana's father's genes had also passed to her. Ever since that had happened, her life had been out of her control.

Which meant? Her mother truly didn't recognize her any longer as far as knowing what Alana's demon half was capable of. Neither did Alana truly understand herself.

"I'm safe, but I have a Matusa demon after me." She couldn't tell her mother where she actually was. She knew her mother would protect her at all costs. But Alana wasn't the only one out there with the ability to control minds. She often wondered why witches and warlocks weren't on the police force more often—to help catch the bad guys. Maybe because if they did use their abilities, strictly humans would suspect them of being unnatural. Sure. Just like they did with human psychics. Although she often wondered if those who had the abilities were actually like her. Well, not exactly like her. Not half demon, anyway. But the witch part instead.

"You know, the bad kind of demon." She wasn't sure her mother remembered that the Matusa were the really bad kind. *"Hunter and Jared are here with me now. We've lost Samson, but we're sure he'll catch up soon. We have a new friend named Celeste."*

"Another demon?" her mother asked, sounding

shocked. Her mother was really with it as far as mothers went. She had to be if she was going to be able to sanely deal with Alana's half demon heritage.

"Yes, but she's going to have to stay clear of us or cause problems with her foster parents. I'll most likely have to leave the area until we can find a way to pin the murder at the zoo on the Matusa who did it."

"Alana," her mother said, her voice choked with emotion.

Alana hated hearing her mother upset. *"I'll be all right, really. On my own, no. But together we can manage this."*

Her mother didn't say anything.

"Momma."

"They're watching the house. The cops are."

"I won't come home. If we have to meet, I'll get in touch with you telepathically."

"Alana..."

"Yeah?"

"You make sure if you stay in a hotel with those boys, you have a room to yourself. All right?"

Alana smiled. *"Yeah, Mom, I will. What happened at the police station? When I vanished?"*

"They had a massive teen hunt at the station. They looked everywhere and were sure I was involved in hiding you somehow. That we had some kind of secret communiqué when you left. They believed you were using some kind of ultra-advanced electronic device that made the policewoman who accompanied you believe

you were with her, but had gone a different direction and escaped. Just like at the zoo."

"And they think I'm guilty."

Her mother didn't respond.

"Okay, well we have to find the Matusa and offer him up as the murderer. It'll be fine. I'll talk to you later. Love ya."

"Love you back, honey. I'm glad you have your friends. Be safe."

Alana closed her eyes and rested more soundly against Hunter's shoulder. She smiled at her mother's words. She wasn't as worried that Alana was facing another devil of a Matusa demon, but that she might share a bed with one of her demon hunter friends. But she truly was a pretty cool mom. What other mother would be glad her daughter had a bunch of demonic friends?

"You spoke to your mother?" Hunter asked quietly.

She looked up at him. "How did you know?"

"You furrowed your brow and had a faraway look in your eyes."

She closed her eyes. "I could have been astral traveling."

"You don't furrow your brows when you do that," Hunter said.

"Oh."

"Is your mother all right?"

"Sure. The house is being watched. I'm sure she realizes that with friends like you, I'll be okay."

Hunter didn't say anything for a while, then he chuckled.

"What?"

"You've never said I could be useful before."

"Don't let it go to your head."

He held her closer and kissed the top of her head.

"She's talking about all of us," Jared piped up.

Alana smiled, but didn't respond.

"Right," Hunter said in a way that meant he didn't believe it at all—at least to his way of thinking. Alana was talking about him, and only him. "We'll have to pick up some things for you, Alana."

Jared shook his head. "My parents will think I'm picking up clothes for a girlfriend. I'd get the third degree and then what will I say?"

He wasn't grouchy about it, like Alana thought he might be, but sounded rather proud that he was the one who always paid the bills. Compliments of extremely wealthy parents who had a spare-no-expense-on-their-adopted-son attitude.

"Just tell them your girlfriend is a gorgeous brown-eyed, blonde named Celeste," Alana said. Heck, if Samson wasn't interested in Celeste, maybe Jared would be.

"Right," Jared said, in an annoyed way.

Celeste pulled into the hospital parking lot and gave Jared an irritated look. "I'd rather date a Matusa." She glanced back at Hunter. "No offense."

"I'd figure you were just a little crazy," Hunter said.

"I was being facetious," Celeste responded.

Hunter gave her a small smile, then began issuing orders. "Okay, you and Jared stay with the car. Alana and I will go into the morgue."

"Do you have one of the demon detectors?" Alana asked Hunter.

"Yeah."

She gave Jared a scowl. "It would have been nice if *I'd* had one at the hotel."

Hunter frowned. "You're right. I was afraid you might try to go after one when you should have been resting. But you should have known the Matusa was nearby. You take mine. Jared, next one is mine."

Jared looked like he was ready to strangle Alana. Not that he didn't care for her, but because he rarely had a say in things. She was sure he would have made her a tracking device eventually. But he was doing all the work, and he wanted to say who got what first. She had to feel a little sorry for him. That was probably her witchy human side thinking though. Her demon side reminded her that he was lower on the demon totem pole of power and that was the way things went down.

She smiled and said, "Thank you, Hunter." And then with raised brows, she said to Jared, "Thanks."

He still looked sulky.

"Be careful," Celeste said. "The police might be there this time."

Yeah. Alana hadn't really thought of that, but she could just see them stationed around the morgue. Did they have an APB out on her? Would they arrest her on the spot?

Most likely.

Another notion made her skin chill in trepidation. What if the Matusa had the notion to go after the summoner's personal effects, if he hadn't already? What if he was there now?

With that awful thought in mind, she and Hunter made their way to the morgue. They found two men inside dressed in scrubs, no police officers, and best of all, no Matusa.

She quickly made the two men forget that Hunter and she shouldn't be there.

"Where are the personal effects for the man who was snake bitten at the zoo?" Alana asked, wanting to get this over with in a hurry. The pungent smell of cleaning solutions and the undercurrent of the smell of death clung gruesomely to the white washed room. Plus, every second they stayed here exposed them to a possible encounter with the police or the summoner's murder.

Both men just stared stupidly at her.

"He was brought in this morning. Snake bite marks. Male. Zoo."

Both men nodded and one retrieved the man's personal effects. Then Alana frowned, rethinking the whole scenario. "Why wouldn't the police have kept these as evidence in their investigation of a murder?"

Neither said anything, as if they were confused by her question.

"Wouldn't these be part of police evidence? Just like his clothes would be?"

"Are these..." Hunter read the name on the driver's license, "Jessup Carter's personal effects?"

Neither man responded. Alana asked the same question only this time, the one said, "No."

"Who said these were the man's personal effects?"

"His brother," the one said.

The other pulled out the sign-out sheet and pointed to the name. "His brother," he said.

Expecting to see the name Carter, Alana blinked. It said: *His brother.* "Let us see the dead man."

The two men pulled back the sheet.

She stared at him. She hadn't seen him in the snake room, but this wasn't the same man pictured on the driver's license.

"Who left these personal effects here, saying they were this man's?" she asked.

"The police," the shorter man said.

"It's a trap," Alana telepathically told Hunter. *"They're waiting to see who might come for the man's things."* She focused on the men. "What is this man's name?"

Hunter's phone began ringing and the men looked startled. Alana hurriedly got their attention as Hunter said, "Thanks. We're leaving now." He grabbed Alana's arm. "Scrub their thoughts or whatever it is you do. We've got to go."

"His name?" Alana asked the men again, not

budging from her speck of washed white tile floor.

"Al Cesierone."

"Address?"

"Alana," Hunter said, sharply, gently tugging at her.

She quickly made the men forget that she and Hunter had been there, then she rushed out of the morgue with Hunter. "What's wrong?"

"Police are headed this way. Someone saw us and thought you looked like the girl in the news."

"Great."

They hurried out a back door that put them on the other side of the building a long ways from the parking lot where they'd entered before, which meant they were a lot farther from Celeste's parked car now, too.

"South side of the building," Hunter said to Jared over the phone. "Hurry." Then he added, "Don't run over anyone."

He kept walking with Alana at a quickened pace, making her nearly run to keep up with his longer stride. He moved away from the hospital, and she knew Jared would direct Celeste toward the Matusa and Kubiteron demons on his laptop demon tracker.

Everything would have been fine. Celeste was in view of them and headed directly for them, when a police officer, shouted, "Alana Fainot! Stop right there!"

CHAPTER 7

Hunter had known it would be a risk to take Alana anywhere, but he'd thought it would be a reasonable risk if they could learn who the dead man was and where he had lived. They had to locate his portal opening device and destroy it.

Now they were faced with the possibility Alana could be arrested and him along with her. Getting out of that mess could be a real nightmare.

He and Alana turned to face what he hoped was just a hospital security officer. A lone security officer attempting to detain her until the cops arrived. If so, she could cast her witch's mind control over him, no problem.

Two police officers were heading for them, and two more patrol cars were driving in their direction.

This was so not good.

"I can't do it," she whispered to Hunter.

The interrogation, he thought she meant. She couldn't face any more of it. What if she astral traveled when she was being questioned this time? He didn't think she could deal with it any further.

But he didn't want to have to do what he planned, either. He would have done anything else if he could have come up with another idea on the spur of the moment. "We have to go to the demon world," he said low for her hearing only.

"Stay right there," one of the police officers said, his hand held up as if he was directing traffic, or telling her not to disappear like she had done before.

"They'll see the portal," she whispered back. "They'll see us vanish into it."

"I can't think of any other way." He glanced back at Celeste and Jared. They'd pulled into a parking lot and were waiting to see what would happen next. "Tell them," Hunter said to Alana. "Tell Celeste and Jared we're going to Seplichus for a short jaunt and will return as soon as we can."

Alana turned to face Celeste and Jared, who were both watching them through the windshield. *"We're going to Seplichus. We'll be back as soon as we're able."*

Celeste's eyes grew huge. No one had probably ever spoken into her mind before. Jared looked just as horrified, but not for the same reason. He started shaking his head and got out of the car.

"No, stay," she telepathically told him.

As soon as he got out, Celeste hurried to join him.

The police officers probably suspected they were all together in this then and didn't move, waiting for backup.

The squad cars pulled up on either side of the police officers as a united force. Hunter frowned at Jared and Celeste as they walked toward them.

"Stay. We'll be back," he said to Jared. Then Hunter raised his hands as if to show the police he was unarmed, spoke the words to summon the portal, and once the blue-green lights shimmered under the gray skies, he seized Alana's hand and pulled her through.

***

Torrential cold rain and winds pelted Hunter and Alana as they stood near a bulkhead that was trying to keep a stormy sea at bay. Alana moved closer to him as rain pelted them from the gray sky above. They were again in the demon world. Only this one was a lot wetter than the others he'd visited.

He hesitated to close the portal as local demons hurrying through the stormy weather headed for shelter. A few glanced in their direction, noticing the portal, and a couple of males instantly gave Alana a second look. They considered Hunter again, a Matusa demon, and hurried on their way.

"Close the portal," Alana said.

He couldn't. Not when they'd left Jared and Celeste behind, and he was certain the police would arrest them. Then what would they say? They'd have no explanation as to what had happened to Hunter and Alana.

Suddenly Jared and Celeste rushed out of the portal, Jared cursing under his breath as they got slammed by the wind and rain.

Frowning at them, Hunter closed the portal, shutting them off from Earth world.

"Ohmigod," Celeste said, her hand clinging to Jared's as she drew even closer to him. "This is it. This is really it."

"Come on," Hunter said, heading away from the bulkhead that was trying to hold back a raging wall of ocean water, the gray from above blending with the dark gray waters, the only other color, a frothing white foam stirred up by the relentless wind. "Let's find a building to wait out the storm."

The temperature was so cold, he felt Alana shivering in his protective embrace. She looked uncomfortable, and he was certain it was because of the experience she'd had when she'd been here before in a Matusa's clutches, while he and Jared had been unable to locate her.

"We are in so much trouble," Celeste said, casting them a half smile.

Seemed as though the Camaran demon was enjoying this adventure. That brought back to mind Jared's description of their demon type—they loved danger.

"You shouldn't have left the car," Alana scolded. "They would never have suspected we were together." Her teeth chattered as she shivered, their clothes soaking straight through.

"Not true," Jared said.

Hunter cast a glance at him. Jared was a real asset. In one regard, Hunter had wanted to leave them safely behind, until Jared and Celeste got out of the car, making it obvious they were with Alana and Hunter. He hadn't wanted them to get involved with the police, although he couldn't deny he hadn't really wanted to leave Jared behind, either. In the time they'd been together, watching each other's backs, protecting each other, they'd been a real team. As for Celeste, he hadn't wanted to pull her into this world. Best if she had stayed out of it all together.

"Why would they have suspected we were together?" Hunter asked gruffly, annoyed. He was supposed to be in charge. *He* made the rules.

"Hospital surveillance cameras. I hadn't thought of that, but once the police saw the two of you, they probably would have discovered the car that you had arrived in. *Celeste's.* She would have been implicated anyway."

Hunter cursed. "All right."

"What do you think the police are doing now?" Celeste asked, snuggling even tighter to Jared.

To Hunter's surprise, Jared actually placed his arm around Celeste and held her tightly against his body as they rushed to reach the first apartment-like building located nearby. Gray brick blended with gray pavement and all the windows were dark as if the electricity had been knocked out.

Before anyone could answer her, Celeste said, "I'm

certain the police are impounding my car, informing my parents, *foster* parents, and getting my profile. Trying to learn just how bad I am."

"How bad are you?" Jared asked, sounding surprised.

She smiled up at him. "I see future visions, remember? That makes me pretty bad."

Alana groaned as Hunter directed them straight to the closest building. "This is Tarn's building. The Baltimore Matusa's," she said in explanation to Celeste who hadn't known about the demon shapershifter who could change his demon aura.

"He still lives here?" Celeste asked.

"No, vacated. Permanently."

"Maybe we could stay at his place," Celeste offered. "Since he's vacated it."

"If he hasn't paid up his rent, he might have been 'moved' out," Alana warned.

Hunter had to agree it was a good idea, although he noted Alana didn't seem thrilled with the prospect, and he couldn't blame her.

They finally managed to get inside the building and found a bank of elevators. No lobby, no management, just a whole lot of elevators. And mirrors. Hunter and the others all looked bedraggled. Sopping wet clothing, straggly wet hair. All of them were shivering.

"Can we operate them?" Celeste asked, wrinkling her nose as she stared at her appearance in a mirror.

"I imagine so," Alana said. "I only saw Tarn do so,

but I'm sure that anyone could."

Jared was already running his hand over a panel, and the doors to the elevator zipped open.

"Hold onto your stomachs," Alana warned as they entered the large compartment. "It goes *really* fast."

"Floor?" Jared asked.

"Fortieth floor," she said, and a disembodied female voice said back, "Fortieth floor."

They all looked up as if some unseen creature would be floating above their heads.

The elevator swished to life, shooting to the requested floor. No music, and the walls were mirrored, making it appear as if twice as many demons were riding the elevator. Above, soft lighting muted the harshness.

"Ohmigod," Celeste said, her mouth gaping, eyes wide, looking as though she was on a roller coaster ride. And she loved it.

Alana looked a little green.

Tension building in every muscle as he prepared himself for battle, Hunter was concerned about what they would find if they tried to enter the Matusa's apartment. What if another had moved in? What if the place was now some other demon's home? A family even? He didn't want to crash in on anyone. If they were Matusa, that was really bad news for them.

Worse, what if Tarn had a relative who had taken over the place? And he learned Hunter had killed him?

"I have to warn you," Alana said, as they left the elevator and entered a hallway, the walls covered in silvery fabric. The indoor-outdoor looking dark gray carpet concealed their footfalls. At the end of the hall, a window looked out on the city, the dark clouds hovering overhead, the rain slanting, pelting the glass as if trying to get in. Dark gray sconces held shimmering candle-like lights that made the hall appear shadowed and gloomy. "Tarn had some nasty poltergeist guards in the apartment. I got rid of the ones that had appeared, but it might not be totally ghost free."

"You can exorcise ghosts?" Celeste asked with genuine awe.

"Yeah," Jared said. "You would not believe all the scary things she can do."

Hunter wasn't sure how to take Jared's comment. Was he impressed? Or still feeling uneasy about her abilities, since they weren't on his chart of Kubiteron powers known to them?

"Yeah, just remember that, Elantus," Alana warned.

He smiled at her.

Hunter frowned. He hoped Jared didn't think that he had a chance with Alana. He would have to change his opinion if that was the case.

When they reached the pale gray door to the apartment, he paused to see no doorknob.

"Panel," Jared said, pointing to the lighted panel on the wall next to the door. "Probably geared to analyze a handprint, so none of us would be able to open it."

Alana pulled out the demon tracker device and switched it on. For a second, the small screen was filled with demon blips, the color surrounding them, indicating their demon type. But there were so many of them, they appeared to be on top of each other. The screen on the device went black.

Hunter stared at the black screen.

"What happened?" Jared asked.

"Your device is broken," Alana said, annoyed.

"Not broken," Jared said. "Probably can't handle so many demon types in one area."

"Your laptop worked in the demon swamps," Alana reminded him.

"Right, because there were so few demons there."

Hunter cleared his throat. "How do we get into the apartment?"

Jared moved forward and pulled a metal tool out of his pocket, then began to take the panel apart. All kinds of red, black, and yellow wires filled the box, and he began fiddling with them.

"Do you know what you're doing?" Hunter asked.

"No. Maybe one of these will bypass the panel recognition device and will allow us to open the door."

"Or?"

"I might accidentally break it."

Hunter rubbed Alana's wet sleeve, trying to warm her up. All of them were shivering, the hall feeling as though it was air conditioned.

After several minutes of no success, Hunter looked around them. The carpet was a motley gray, the walls a silver shimmery fabric, and the doors all slate gray. None of the doors had numbers on them. If a demon ever got drunk, how would he find the right apartment?

Hunter moved Alana over to the window to look out at the storm-besieged city and decide where to go next.

"What are we going to do if we can't get into the apartment?" she asked.

"We need to open another portal, but we've got to get a lot farther away or we'll end up just reappearing near the hospital parking lot. Police will probably be in the area for hours, trying to locate us."

"They'll tell Mom. Probably question her again as to what kind of devices we have that are causing me, and you and the others now, to vanish in full view."

"We could eventually make our way back to Dallas and take a portal to the demon city where the hall of records is," Jared said, still pulling wires apart and reconnecting them.

"We're a long way from there," Hunter countered.

"The police don't have a clue as to who we are, yet. We could go to my parent's home. They're on another cruise—world this time. I'm always welcome to crash there anytime, my friends included."

"Friends" meant Hunter as Jared didn't easily make friends. He didn't fit in with others his age, partly because of his electronic tinkering. Not to mention the problem with being a full demon and not quite into the regular human scene.

"We could do that," Hunter conceded. "But we're still a long way from Dallas here, and trying to move across the demon world safely to get to a location where we could open a portal to Earth world would probably be impossible."

"How can you open a portal?" Celeste suddenly asked. "Demons can't, or they'd be on Earth world all over the place."

"Our human half can do it," Alana said.

"Oh."

A door swished open on the other side of the hall and everyone turned to look.

A Matusa. Hunter quickly shoved Alana, the Matusa demon magnet, behind him as he took up a fighting stance. He wondered now if this whole complex wasn't inhabited by Matusa. In fact, that might be so. Would other demons fear living across the hall from a Matusa?

Unless because of his demon shifting power, Tarn had hidden what he was.

Still, what were the odds that another Matusa would live across the hall otherwise?

"Friends of Tarn?" the man said, his black eyes taking in Jared's attempt to access the door opener panel, Celeste, standing near him, Hunter, the only real threat to another Matusa, and Alana, a spark igniting in his eyes as he got a glimpse of her.

"Yeah, friends of his," Alana said, and Hunter wished she'd be quiet and keep in the background as much as possible. Although he should have known she wouldn't.

"Really." A dark smile curved the Matusa's lips.

"Yeah, he had a poltergeist problem, and I helped to get rid of them for him."

At that, the Matusa gave a sharp bark of laughter. Then he studied her more carefully, his expression one of resolution. "You will do, Kubiteron."

Jared grabbed Celeste's arm and yanked her away from the Matusa, moving her quickly in the opposite direction of Hunter and Alana.

Hunter knew Jared did so not because he was afraid. But because he knew Hunter and the Matusa were getting ready to fight, and Hunter needed room to maneuver.

"Hand her over," the Matusa said smoothly to Hunter, "and I won't alert Tarn's brother that you're here, trying to break into Tarn's place."

Tarn *would* have to have a brother. Sometimes they avenged their family's deaths. Sometimes they didn't. So Hunter had no idea whether it would matter or not to Tarn's brother. Well, and then, too, he probably wouldn't know that Tarn was dead, had died, on Earth world. Because of them.

Hunter also knew that if the brother had known Tarn wanted Alana, he probably would be happy to take his place.

"We don't want any trouble," Hunter said, knowing that any fight he engaged in could have disastrous results for any of them.

"You won't get any, if you move along and leave the Kubiteron here, with me."

Alana moved around Hunter and cast a spell to open a portal in the hallway before he could stop her.

The demon looked at it, and then back at her. "How did you…" He glanced back at the portal.

Hunter shook his head. "Now I've got to kill him."

The demon cast him an evil smile. "Bring her to me later." Then he stepped into the portal, and Alana quickly shut it.

Hunter swore. "I'm the Matusa. I'm in charge. When are you going to ever get that straight?" He grabbed her hand and began hauling her toward the open apartment the Matusa had just vacated.

"Oh, I remember. You are the big, bad Matusa." When she smiled up at him and wrapped her arm around his waist, what could he do?

But shake his head again.

"Wow," Celeste said, hurrying to join Hunter and Alana as they entered the apartment, Jared following behind. "I figured there'd be this horrendous fight and we'd all be at risk, and then, what a great solution," she said to Alana.

The door slid closed.

"Not a great solution," both Hunter and Alana said at one time.

"The Matusa is now in our world," Alana said. "I couldn't think of any other way to get rid of him. It was either fight him and risk the rest of us getting injured, or offer him something he might like even more. A way into Earth world."

"He didn't look like he was ready to give you up either," Celeste said.

"He isn't," Hunter said. "Which means when we return to Baltimore, we'll have to either send him back here, or kill him. Now that makes two of them."

"We still have to find the portal opener," Jared said. "So even if we want to avoid returning to Baltimore, we really have no choice."

"I wonder if he's got a clothes dryer in here," Celeste said, wringing out the hem of her dress.

A knock at the door made them all turn around to stare at it as if their movements were choreographed.

Hunter stalked over to the door and looked through a panel that he hadn't seen on the outside of the doors. Some kind of visitor viewing device that wouldn't permit the viewee to see the viewer?

The demon standing before the door looked a hell of a lot like Tarn. His brother. *Had to be.* So, the Matusa living here must have called Tarn's brother already. *Liar.* Not that Hunter was all that surprised. Except to see the Matusa already standing before the door.

"Pennel!" the Matusa said, then looked back at the mess Jared had made of the door opener panel to his brother's apartment. He turned his stormy gray attention to Pennel's door again and said, "Pennel! Open up."

It appeared that the demon couldn't access Pennel's apartment, though when he stalked over to his brother's door, it looked like he couldn't make it work either. He faced Pennel's apartment, pulled out something that looked like a communication device of some sort, and spoke into it, "Pennel? Where the hell are you? I'm here, at your apartment. The Elantus isn't here. Nor... what was it that you said the other was? A Camaran demon? Why would they try to break into Tarn's apartment? They know they would have been killed for it. No other demon types in their right mind would have entered a Matusa living complex even."

That's what Hunter had belatedly figured—that the whole place was full of Matusa. Which meant they probably couldn't just walk out of here without a fight if anyone had noticed Alana enter the building.

Tarn's brother paused, glowered at the door, then said, "Call me back as soon as you get this message."

Then he stalked off down the hall.

No one said a word, all of them probably concerned their voices might carry.

Then Alana let out her breath. "Now what?"

"We still can't return to the parking lot at the hospital. At least when you opened the portal, we were far enough from the original location when we first appeared in the demon's world that it won't be that close to the hospital when Pennel arrived. So, hopefully, he didn't encounter the police." Hunter snorted. "I wonder if the hospital cameras were able to pick up the lights of the portal when we went through it. Or if anyone might have captured what had happened on a cell phone. I can just see us all featured on Youtube. But we still need to get farther away from the original site."

"We'll need a car," Celeste said, disappearing into another room.

"We can't take yours," Hunter said, wondering what she was up to.

"There's some kind of a drying machine in here," Celeste said. "At least I think so. Maybe Jared could figure out how to work it."

"Or make a mess of it," Jared said, sounding annoyed with himself for not being able to get into Tarn's apartment.

"Probably just as well we didn't get in there," Hunter said. "Pennel had been watching us, or at least he saw you and Celeste, but must not have been alerted to our presence for a while and by then Alana and I were standing at the end of the hall at the window where he couldn't see us. Since he had alerted Tarn's brother, we would have been in Tarn's apartment when his brother arrived."

"Yeah, that's true," Jared said, playing around with some kind of machine that looked like a large microwave. "Get a shirt or something of Pennel's wet, and we'll experiment, Celeste."

She found a shirt, took it into a washroom, got it soaking wet, and brought it back to Jared.

He shoved it into the "dryer," then closed the door, and tried a setting. Nothing happened. He tried another button and the shirt began to smoke.

"It's on fire," Celeste said, her eyes wide.

"No, it's steam."

Before their eyes, the shirt turned from dark, wet blue, to light blue, perfectly water-free fabric.

Celeste said, "Wow, that was fast."

"Start stripping," Jared said to everyone. "I'll dry our clothes off in a jiff."

Celeste laughed. "That's a guy line if I ever heard one." She left the room and returned minus her dress, while she was now wearing an oversized black men's shirt.

Alana hurried into the same room and came back wearing Pennel's black robe. Hunter couldn't help the surge of irritation that made him feel. He didn't like it that she was wearing anything of the Matusa's. If the man ever did make it back here alive, he'd know the Kubiteron had been wearing his clothes and would want her all the more. Her unique scent would be imprinted on his memory forever, like it was on Hunter's.

After they had dried their clothes and redressed, they checked out the kitchen where Celeste started opening cabinets while Hunter took the robe Alana had borrowed, filled a basin with water, and threw the garment into the water. After pouring a strange smelling liquid into the water, he turned to see Alana watching him, curious as to what he was up to.

"Figure we shouldn't wear someone else's clothes without washing them for him afterward," he said.

"Yeah, and that's why you're washing *only* the robe that I had worn?"

Hunter gave her a devilish smile.

She shook her head.

"Do you feel all right? Being here, I mean," he asked.

"Now that we know we're in a whole tower complex of Matusa demons?"

"They must be out or sleeping, or busy in their apartments and not watching out the windows, or I'm sure we would have had trouble when we first arrived," Hunter said.

"Eww," Celeste said from the kitchen. "What is this stuff?" She pulled out a clear container of something gray and squishy looking.

"Demon food," Alana said. "Tarn told me he had gotten both demon and human food for me, my choice. Well, and probably for the warlock who was working for him. He wouldn't have been able to stomach demon food, either."

"Did you try any of it?" Celeste asked.

"No. I was busy exorcising ghosts and trying to figure a way out of his apartment. I'm sure if we had been raised on demon food, human food would not seem very appealing, either."

Celeste snorted. "If I'd ever harbored any crazy idea of living in the demon world, this would have killed that notion in a hurry. Although I am starving. It's nearly dinner time and we never even had lunch today."

"So what do we do?" Jared asked. "Transport out of here where it's nice and dry and we'll end up close to where Pennel showed up in Baltimore, not far from the hospital? Or go back out into that hurricane-like weather—or try to. We may not be able to leave this building. Or even if we do, we might not get very far."

"Can you control demon's minds?" Celeste asked Alana.

"No."

"So what do we do, Hunter?" Jared again asked.

CHAPTER 8

Life as a demon hunter was one calculated risk.
Hunter always tried to take the least amount of risk in a
situation that involved Jared or Alana. Faced with
Celeste's safety also now, he had to really make the right
choice this time.

He finally said, "Tarn's brother was too complacent
when he left here."

"Meaning?" Jared asked.

"He suspects foul play. Pennel never answered his
phone. Why not? The demons trying to break into Tarn's
apartment had conveniently disappeared. Where to?"
Hunter said.

"So he's lying in wait for us?" Jared asked.

"Or getting hold of the authorities to report the
break-in, and maybe even share his concern with them
that Pennel has been injured or taken hostage in his own
apartment."

"By the brute force of an Elantus and Camaran demon?" Jared asked. "He'd be laughed out of the security forces building."

"He may improvise and say a couple of Matusa had done so. It would seem more likely."

"So you believe we should open a portal here, return to Baltimore, and chance running into the police?" Jared said.

"Wait!" Alana said, her expression stricken. "I might have killed him!"

Hunter stared at her, uncomprehending.

"I opened the portal at forty stories above street level."

Everyone gaped at her, then Hunter smiled. "Good, then Pennel shouldn't be a problem. Too bad we couldn't have somehow pinned the summoner's murder on him until we could locate that Matusa."

Alana rubbed her arms and Hunter noticed the chill bumps on them. He pulled her close. "I know you didn't mean to do it."

"He would have killed you and Jared for sure."

Hunter grunted. "He could have tried."

"I only meant to get rid of him in the interim."

"Yeah, well, now we have a new problem. We've got to get to the ground floor of this building, then open a portal."

"I should have thought it out better," Alana said, sounding miserable.

"Are you upset that you probably killed him?"

"No, not exactly, because it would have come to that eventually, but I should have... *known*."

"We all should have considered it. At least you came to the realization well before *we* used the portal ourselves. Are we all agreed that we try to make it to the first floor and then open the portal?"

"When the warlock, Connor, and I tried to escape Tarn's place, we used a mattress I levitated until we could reach the ground."

"No, we're not going that way. If you could even do such a thing with all of us, by the time we reached the ground, I could see us surrounded by Matusa and security forces."

She nodded. "We couldn't leave the apartment any other way. Our only choice was to break out the window."

That notion gave his heart a jumpstart. He didn't even want to think of what might have happened if she'd lost her concentration while levitating them to safety.

Celeste moved to the door and looked through the rectangular viewing panel. "Looks clear," she said. "But I can't see all the way to the ends of the hall."

"We don't have any choice," Hunter said. "Are we all ready?"

They all nodded in silent agreement, and Hunter opened the door. He looked down each side of the hall. "All clear," he whispered. Then he added, "Women in the middle. Jared, you follow up from behind."

Once he realized Alana's assumption was right and

they had only two choices at this point—reach the ground floor and either head into the bad weather or open a portal first—he was ready to make a move. He prayed the way would remain clear.

***

Celeste was fascinated with how Alana, Hunter, and Jared worked as a team. Even though Hunter was clearly in charge, he had his moments when he let the others apply their own wits and skills to solve a problem. She only wished she'd have some vision of a future event that might help them. Unfortunately, they were totally unpredictable and so nothing was forthcoming.

Though she was terrified of having to face a score of angry Matusa in the complex, she couldn't help the thrill of excitement buzzing through her veins. She always knew she was weird.

She'd never thought of herself as a thrill-seeker. But maybe Jared was right that Camaran demons loved to face danger.

She glanced back at Jared. He was stony-faced, but appeared to be ready for any eventuality. Alana walked tall and straight and appeared as though she was solemnly contemplating what they might face. Hunter moved like a warrior, forcefully, determined, yet carefully, quietly, more like a panther than a soldier stomping on the ground, letting everyone know he was ready to face his enemy head on.

They were nearly to the elevators when a door opened to one of the apartments behind them.

Neither Alana or Hunter looked back. Did they not hear the door open behind them? She turned her head and saw a Matusa child watching them, incredulity in her expression, chilling but beautiful black eyes studying her. Celeste was certain they didn't have visitors to the tower who were not Matusa demons. And that's just what was going through the little girl's mind.

The girl said nothing. Maybe she was afraid of them. Or maybe she was afraid of what her father might do to them if he saw them. Maybe that would ruin her outing with him today. Though what a day to go on an outing.

Jared frowned at Celeste, and she had the distinct impression he wanted her to turn around and pretend the little girl wasn't there.

"Lisalee, return and put on your rain cloak," a gruff male voice said inside the apartment.

She smiled at Celeste, but the look was pure evil. As if to say she'd give them a head start, then the chase was on.

Sure enough, as soon as Hunter pressed the elevator button, the Matusa child said, "Daddy, are any other kinds of demons supposed to be on our floor?"

The elevator reached their floor and opened. A middle-aged male Matusa stood inside. Hunter was the first to react. The man bowed his head a little in greeting to Hunter, but then he saw the other demons behind him. The Matusa's eyes grew round, and Hunter leapt forward, kicking him in the belly, yelling, "In," to his companions. He judo chopped the man in the throat, making him gasp for air.

Then he tossed the Matusa out of the elevator. The Matusa went sprawling on his belly. From inside the elevator, Celeste watched as the girl shook her finger at them as if to say they had been naughty. Just as the doors began to shut, she said, "Well, Daddy, the lesser demons just threw Hirolson off the elevator."

Which wasn't true. Hunter had done the job. Celeste figured the child would get more of a reaction if she said a lesser demon had dared to beat up a fellow Matusa.

The doors whispered shut and Hunter pulled Alana into his embrace and kissed her. "Be ready for anything." He added, "This isn't going to be easy, Celeste. If you can help in any way, do your best."

"I will." But she wasn't sure how she could help.

As fast as the elevator had ascended before, she thought it would descend just as quickly, but about halfway to the ground floor, it suddenly stopped. She looked up. Floor twenty-one.

Her skin chilled and she moved away from the door. She wished that she could do something to help. She wished Alana could wipe the Matusa demons' minds and make them believe the occupants of the elevator were all Matusa like them.

The doors slid open and three male Matusa stood staring at them, not moving into the elevator, just looking from one to the next.

"What the hell's going on?" one of the men said, then pinned his gaze on Alana, though Hunter had moved protectively in front of her. "Well, *hello*, Kubiteron," he added in a roughly seductive voice.

Forgotten for the moment, Celeste figured it was her turn to do something brave and heroic. She moved toward the button, but something was in her way. A body, but nothing was visible. She glanced back where Jared should have been, but he was gone.

The close door button was depressed, the doors whisked shut, and the elevator shot downward. Pounding on the outer doors could be heard from way up above.

"Jared?" Celeste asked.

He reappeared in front of her and smiled.

"You can become invisible," Celeste said, with a real sense of wonderment.

"Yeah. I would have done so earlier, like when you and I got out of your car to join Hunter and Alana, but I was afraid I'd shake you up too much. I only do it when I think there's a real advantage to it."

"Cool," she said, wishing she could do something like that.

Although she didn't think any of the Matusa could make it down in another elevator any faster than they were going, she reconsidered when the elevator slowed and stopped again. She glanced up and groaned. Floor six. Still too many feet from the ground to risk using a portal. Probably close to sixty feet. They'd all be broken to smithereens if Hunter opened a portal now, and they entered it.

The door slid open. A Matusa female carrying a

baby stared at the demons. "What are you—"

"Wrong building, ma'am," Jared said politely, stepping forward, then closed the door in her face.

"We're almost there," Alana said, but spoke the words too soon.

The elevator jerked to a stop at the next floor down. At this rate, the three male Matusa would make it to the first floor before they got there. A scrawny little boy was already heading away from the elevator when he turned to give them a sassy look. Then his jaw dropped as he saw all the different demon types, and he tore off.

"Maybe he's pressing the elevator buttons to pull a prank on passengers," Hunter said.

"Good. Then that'll stop the three men, too," Celeste said, hopefully. "But bad in that he'll probably report us to his parents."

"They still had to wait for an elevator also, which will help slow them down a bit," Jared added. "I'm sure we'll get to the ground floor before anyone else can try to stop us."

They moved past the fourth and third floor with no problem and Alana said, "When we get to the ground floor, press the closed button and—"

The elevator stopped at floor two. The doors opened, and Tarn's brother and three other men stood in the hall looking at Celeste. "I'm Fasino, Tarn's brother. You must be the ones who tried to pay him a visit. He hasn't been home in a while. Do you know where he's gone?" He glanced at Hunter and frowned. "Pennel didn't say anything about a Matusa or a... *my*. What have we *here*? Pennel failed to mention *you*."

Celeste nearly laughed. Even though Jared had told her that male demons were attracted to the Kubiteron, she hadn't believed him.

She reached out to push the button to close the door, but Fasino grabbed her wrist, and she squeaked. He gave her a wicked smile. "You will do for one of my friends."

He tossed her to one of the other men who wrapped his meaty arms around her waist and held on tight, but as soon as he did, he released her and clutched at his heart, an anguished cry stuck in his throat.

Fasino went after Hunter, the only real threat to any of the Matusa, but Alana suddenly raised her fingers and said some kind of a spell, and he began to elevate off the floor. Then he flew into the other two men, and an invisible hand grabbed Celeste and pulled her into the elevator. She slammed her hand against the down button, hoping Jared was in the elevator.

Fasino had knocked the two men off their feet as the one with the heart problems was writhing on the floor in pain.

When they reached the first floor, Celeste kept her finger on the door close button to keep it from opening. Alana summoned a portal and the four of them jumped through it, landing on top of each other in a tumble of arms and legs in a grassy park, a short distance from the hospital. Hunter quickly closed the portal, and Celeste hoped no one saw it.

Alana said, "Ohmigod, there's Pennel."

She was still on her back on the ground as Hunter rose to help her up. She was staring at a nearby tree. They all looked up and Celeste saw him, too, hanging in the branches, broken, dead.

No one else must have seen him yet.

"Too bad we still couldn't plant incriminating evidence on him so that you would be cleared of any wrongdoing," Hunter said, helping Alana to her feet.

"What now?" Jared asked, looking around.

Celeste then noticed a group of walkers on a trail staring at them.

Seeing them, too, Hunter said, "We move, fast."

That's when the air grew frosty, and Alana said, "Indigo."

A mist swirled about them next, and she smiled. "Samson," she whispered.

Celeste stared at the frosty mist in their hair and shivered.

"The gang's together again. Let's go," Hunter reiterated. "Jared, get us a taxi, quick."

***

After wiping the driver's mind of having given four demons a ride in his taxi, along with a frigid cold presence in the back seat—although Hunter had told Indigo to take a hike—and a mist that surrounded all of them, they were now back at the hotel room.

"Pizza?" Celeste asked. "I'm starving."

Samson turned the television on and was watching

the news. Paranormal crews had come in from all over the States to analyze the photographs and video taken at the hospital to determine if real paranormal activity had taken place.

Everyone stared at the television. "We all look so grim faced," Jared said. "We should have smiled for the camera."

"I had to watch this all day while I awaited your return to the area," Samson said sourly.

Hunter took Alana's hand and moved her to the bed. "You never got your rest, did you?"

She shook her head. As soon as she climbed onto the bed, he sat next to her and cuddled.

Indigo made a chilling pass over them, and Hunter scowled. "I will learn how to exorcise ghosts before long, Matusa. Count on it."

"Order some pizza for us, Jared. I'm hungry, too," Alana said.

"The Matusa knows Alana's staying here," Samson said, his tone of voice still grumpy. He gave Hunter a dirty look. "How could you have taken Alana to the morgue and nearly gotten her arrested?"

"We discovered the name of the summoner," Hunter said, stroking Alana's hair.

She closed her eyes and snuggled closer to him.

"So why aren't we going to his place?" Samson asked.

"Police are probably watching it," Hunter said.

"Oh." Samson changed the channel to another

breaking news story.

Alana didn't mind him switching channels now, not with Hunter here. She felt calm and relaxed for the first time since her ordeal at the zoo.

A news commentator said, "Unidentified man found dead in tree in park near hospital. Cause of death unknown."

"Pennel," Alana said quietly.

The newsman said, "Authorities say eyewitnesses have allegedly seen more blue-green lights in the park."

Grainy film capturing the portal lights appeared on the news report and then four people all tangled together on the ground suddenly materialized.

Alana groaned as she watched her camera version self look up at the tree where Pennel had fallen, and then the others with her had all looked that way.

"Walkers in the area said the group of two women and two men walked off in a southerly direction. Police are still searching for them.

"In other news—"

Samson clicked the controller and found a channel where paranormal investigators on a panel were discussing the situation in Baltimore.

"In paranormal investigations, we use the very latest of paranormal investigative equipment that in laymen's terms can locate hot and cold spots and electronic magnetic impulses, the thermal imaging camera, EMF radiation reader and temperature readings. If you look closely at this video tape, you can see the man and woman were headed straight into the shimmering lights. You would expect they would walk right through them and we'd see them on the other side of the lights. But they didn't. As if to prove what we had seen, another couple joined them. They vanished as if going through a doorway. Then the doorway shut, and the opening was gone. You can observe where the police walked all over the same spot where the lights had been, and nothing was there any longer."

"It's a fake," another expert on the paranormal said. "You can see by the way the lights waver, it's not really uniform as it would be for a stable opening to any other reality. The first girl and guy don't step into it as if they're walking through a doorway, but move as if it's an optical illusion. You can see the way their feet don't quite go into the opening. When the person or persons tampered with this film, they missed fixing that oversight."

"You're saying that the dozen or so spectators either happening to glance out the hospital windows and curiously watch what the police officers were doing in the parking lot, or visitors or employees or patients who were leaving or going to their parked cars witnessed the blue green lights as one big hoax?"

"What I'm saying is that people will see what they want to see. There was an atmospheric shift in the weather, the odd cold air mixed with warmer air, the shimmering projection off both people and lights made everyone who saw the spectacle believe they'd witnessed some alien activity. It's a form of mass hysteria. You can't deny there are reports all over the world of sudden blue green lights appearing and people disappearing into them."

"I beg to disagree. In my estimation, these are beings from another planet who have disguised themselves to look like humans. The occurrences are genuine and if we neglect to consider them as such, the human race could be put in harm's way."

Alana shook her head.

Samson switched the channel to another news site, while Jared asked everyone what kind of toppings and pizza crust they wanted.

"Since you came from the demon world," Celeste said, pulling up a chair next to Samson, "how did your food compare with ours?"

"It's different," he said. "Different tastes, textures, appearance. But just as good."

"We saw some gray squishy stuff in Pennel's fridge. What would that have been?"

"Sounds like squib. A delicacy. Tastes like shrimp and brown gravy." Samson said again to Hunter, "What about Thorst? He knows Alana is staying here."

"He's welcome to pay her a visit. Anytime."

The news commentator said, "In other news, one of the girls who allegedly vanished into the lights this afternoon was Celeste Sweetwater. She and Alana Fainot were the only two that police could positively identify. If anyone knows of their whereabouts, the police hotline number is scrolling at the bottom of the screen."

"I wonder if my parents are watching this," Celeste said glumly.

"*Foster* parents," Jared reminded her.

"Where's everyone sleeping tonight?" Samson asked.

Hunter said, "That bed is mine." He pointed to the other queen-sized bed. "Alana and Celeste will share this bed. You and Jared can get roll-out beds."

Celeste smiled at Hunter. "If you want to stay with Alana, I'll share a bed with either Samson or Jared. As long as neither snore."

"No," Hunter said.

Alana patted his chest. "He's a Matusa. He gets his own bed. Most of the time."

"Yeah, well, it won't always be that way," he said, giving her a smug look. "But while we're all together, that's how it'll be."

"Pizza order's in. What's next on the agenda?" Jared asked.

Hunter thought about it for a moment, then said, "You and Samson are going to the summoner's house."

"You said the police will be there," Jared said.

"Yes. You can become invisible, and Samson can slip in under the door in the form of mist."

"I could go and if the police are there, I could make them forget I'm there," Alana said.

Hunter shook his head. "No. If there are too many of them, or if they have surveillance cameras in place, you'd be identified once again. We can't afford them tying you into any more of this. On the other hand… you can convince a taxi driver that none of us exist, so we'll commandeer the transportation for the mission and wait for Jared and Samson."

And hoped they didn't get in any deeper over this whole muddled Matusa mess than they were already in.

***

Later that night when everything was dark, Jared and Samson arrived at the summoner's house, courtesy of Alana and Hunter getting a taxi for them. Alana had the taxi driver stop at the next street over, then ensured he would forget he was even there as they waited. Hopefully, everyone in the housing development was asleep, and no one would call the police about a taxi sitting idly on their street when it shouldn't be.

Samson couldn't see Jared, but he figured Jared could see the strange misty trail that was Samson as they hurried to the summoner's house on the next street.

A patrol car sat curbside, and two policemen sat inside drinking coffee.

"Around back," Jared whispered.

He and Jared slipped over a fence and hurried across the junky backyard filled with rusting lawn furniture and dead plants in clay pots on the patio while the grass was knee-high. The teacher definitely didn't have a green thumb or an interest in yard maintenance.

When they reached the back door, Samson sifted under the door, glad that so many buildings were not weather sealed like they ought to be, then shifted into his physical form and unlocked and opened the door for Jared. Jared stepped inside, or at least Samson thought he had since he couldn't see or hear him, then he shut the door and returned to his mist form, just in case cameras had been installed to keep up surveillance on the inside of the house. Although he doubted it would be.

Samson moved to the hallway, unsure which direction Jared was going to go. Then he slipped into an office, looked around to see if any cameras were watching what he was doing. Seeing none, he shifted again. He searched through desk drawers and files in a cabinet, examined pieces of equipment that might have been used to build a portal device, but he didn't see anything that might be the actual device. Jared would probably know more about what he was looking for though.

After searching through the office and finding nothing, he moved to a master bedroom. The bed was unmade, plastic cups and plates and sacks from various fast food places littered the bedside table. The summoner had been a slob.

Samson didn't find anything in any of the drawers, closet, or under the bed. He turned and ran into a solid invisible object. "Jared?" he said, his heart racing.

"Nothing in the house," Jared whispered. "Let's check the attached garage."

The two moved that way, Jared opening the door, then they stepped inside. The place was a cluttered mess of a mountain-sized stack of electronic gizmos. No room for a vehicle to park in here.

Jared whistled. "I could have a field day here."

"Yeah, well, all we're looking for is the portal device."

"I have a feeling it's not here," Jared said, moving pieces of metal aside to uncover a myriad of electronic devices.

"Why do you say that?"

"He had to be using it at the zoo."

"Yeah, but it was projected from somewhere, and if so where else would it have been?"

"Someplace close to the zoo? On the zoo premises? I don't know." Jared lifted a device, black metal, the size of a bread box. "Hmm, this might be what we were looking for."

"How could it have gotten under all that junk when he was projecting at the zoo and was found dead there?"

"I believe this might be an earlier device. Which, if in the wrong hands, might be used to make a new device."

"Does it work?"

Jared considered all the different colored wires attached to nodes and played around with them, connecting, disconnecting and reconnecting them for a quarter of an hour, then a portal suddenly formed. He smiled. "Yep, it works."

Alana unexpectedly materialized next to the portal and smiled at them. "You found it."

Jared closed his gaping mouth. "I hate it when you do that." He turned off the portal opener. "It's not the one he used." He frowned at her. "Why are you still here? You're supposed to return to the taxi once the portal is closed."

"Seems I can hang around longer, even if I don't want to. Bring it with you. We'll destroy it." She vanished.

"It looks like she can control her astral abilities to some degree now," Samson said, in an admiring way.

"Ha! She has as much control over it as—"

Flashlights headed toward the garage. Samson moved to the window. "Police," he whispered. "They must have seen the portal lights through the window."

"Great," Jared said. "We've got to take this with us. But not right this second." He hid it under some of the junk, then vanished.

Samson shifted into mist, just as the door opened to the house. Running footfalls headed for the garage. The door into the garage slammed open and banged against the wall. "Don't anyone move!"

Samson slipped under some metal junk. He had no idea where Jared was. The police officers stared at the unoccupied room, mouths agape. One jerked up a light switch and a florescent bulb shuddered awake.

"This is just too weird," the one policeman said, holstering his gun while the other switched off his flashlight.

"Yeah, well, you called it in. I said we should wait

until we really found out if anything was here. The guys will really rib us about this."

Police lights flashed outside the windows as three patrol cars drove into the driveway.

Samson cursed inwardly. They had to get the device out of here, but the police would probably be here forever, trying to learn what had caused the blue-green lights to appear.

Six policemen entered the garage, one of them saying, "Where is it? Don't tell me it just vanished."

"We saw it through the window," one of the men said.

"Well? Where is it now?"

Another said, "What have you been drinking in that coffee of yours, Smithers?"

Several chuckled.

"Coffee, Hedrow. We saw what we saw. What the other guys saw in the hospital parking lot. What the maintenance man saw at the zoo. We can't all be crazy."

"Speak for yourself."

"Okay, spread out. Search the garage and see if you can find anything that would have projected the lights."

The men began moving pieces of equipment, fiddling with knobs and buttons, but nothing produced the light.

Annoyed he'd have to keep moving as he was sure the policeman would wonder why mist existed in pockets underneath the equipment, Samson slipped underneath a jagged piece of metal, hoping to get to the door and outside.

Then a policeman came straight for that piece of metal. Hell. If he lifted it, he would see a strange mist. Samson had nowhere else to go. Nowhere else to slide off to without the policeman seeing him.

The light switch cut off.

Samson fled the dark garage through the open door to the house.

"Someone cut the power!" one of the men shouted.

Flashlights sent streams of light all over the room. One of them tried the switch. "Someone turned the light off."

All the men looked around at each other. No one had been near the light switch. *Jared. Had to have been. Good job!*

Samson slipped out of the house, hating to have to leave the device behind, but then he figured he'd try and wait out the police. He had to at least make sure they didn't leave with the portal device.

He settled into a prickly hedge next to the back of the garage and waited.

Jared whispered from somewhere nearby, though he was still invisible. "Samson, are you still here?"

Samson sifted into his human shape, crouched behind the shrubs, the sharp teeth of the glossy leaves scratching his arms. "Here," Samson said in a hushed tone of voice.

Jared didn't speak for a moment as he must have been moving toward him. Then he said right next to him,

"I figure we'll wait and see if they discover the device."

"If they do? What then?"

"We improvise," Jared said. "Hunter's usually the one with the plans, but we're on our own this time."

"They'll wonder what's taking so long," Samson said, wishing they could get word to Alana and Hunter somehow.

"They probably saw the police lights flashing as they drove into the area and know it had to do with us," Jared said.

Samson considered the problem for a moment. "Yeah. I could go and let Alana and Hunter know what we're up to, but if I leave you by yourself and you have to stop the police from taking the device from here, you might not manage on your own."

"So we both stay, watch, wait and oh... no..."

Samson shifted back into his mist form, moved to the window, and peered inside. Two men were looking at the earlier portal device.

"Don't touch anything!" one of the policemen said.

"If we can activate the lights, we'll know we've got the projector," another said. "Otherwise we could take this back and find it won't be what we're looking for and have to start all over again."

One of the men said, "A truck's coming to pick up all this stuff. The earlier sweep through here didn't reveal any connection with what had happened at the zoo, but with the lights going off in here, that's a different story."

Samson and Jared had to act now. Or would it be

easier to ride with the portal device inside the truck? Then what? Once the device arrived at the police station, even more police officers would be there. Plus, Samson and Jared's ride was here.

"We grab it as soon as they've deposited it in the truck and they're busy getting the other stuff," Jared said.

Unless someone remains with the truck, Samson thought.

"Come on. Let's go," Jared said urgently.

Samson moved around to the front of the house, sifting through shrubs until he was in view of the direction the police truck would probably take.

"I'm thinking the guy who murdered the victim might have been trying to steal his technology," a policeman said, as the others gathered in the front lawn to wait for the truck. "Who would have thought a high school science teacher would have been involved in anything so strange?"

"For some criminal purpose. Somehow, he projects his lights and an image of people, then makes them disappear. You know what I think?"

"What?"

"I think it's a distraction. While everyone's concentrating on the colorful lights and projected images, making the viewer believe that the people are there, a crime is being committed."

"Sure. I doubt anyone would look away from the strange lights while they were on. For several seconds afterward, while everyone waited for the lights to reappear, everyone's attention would still be on the spot."

A police truck drove up and parked and everyone greeted the driver. The policemen began to haul the equipment from the garage out to the truck. Although men were walking back and forth, gathering the stuff and depositing it in the vehicle, Samson easily slipped into the bed of the truck and located the device. Just as he headed for it, the device rose and started to float toward him. Samson smiled inwardly.

As Jared carried the device out of the truck, Samson cloaked it in heavy mist. Hopefully, no one could see the device floating in the air. Jared ducked around the front of the truck, obscuring the policemen's view of what he was doing. Whenever Jared moved the device in a direction Samson hadn't anticipated, the object was exposed, again looking as though it was floating in midair.

Still invisible, Jared headed across the street, continuing to use the truck as a way to block the policemen's view of the device as the men continued to load equipment into the truck. Jared was going in the wrong direction though, if they were to take the device to the taxi where Hunter and Alana waited for them on the street behind the summoner's house.

"Hey!" one of the policemen shouted. "Where's that device I put in here?"

"What?"

"It's gone! It was right there. Now it's not there."

"Search the area! Spread out! Whoever took it can't have gotten far."

No, Samson thought morosely. Definitely not far enough.

CHAPTER 9

The policemen began to gather, then quickly moved out, canvassing the area.

The device began to move much more quickly, and Samson assumed Jared was running. In the wrong direction! Samson was just trying to keep up as his misty form floated after Jared.

Then a gate to a backyard swung open and shut. Trees and shrubs filled the backyard, but the most outstanding feature was a green treehouse built onto one of the larger trees. That's exactly where Jared headed. What the devil?

Jared was up the steps and into the low-ceiling room in a jiff. Furnished with a plastic covered pink kid-sized sofa, a treasure chest, a pint-sized wooden table and three chairs, one with a wobbly leg, the house was perfect for children, but Samson imagined Jared was crouched over as he moved the object into the house.

Then he slid the device under the couch. Jared reappeared in his visible form, yanked his cell phone out of his pocket, and punched in a number. "We've got the device, Hunter. We're at 1306 Olive but the police are scouring the area for us."

"All right, I'm consulting Mapquest. Hold on." Hunter came back on and said, "A river is two miles northeast of your location. Dump it in the river."

"Are you certain?"

"Yeah, we don't want the police or anyone else to get hold of it. Then we'll come for you, using the demon tracker."

"All right," Jared said. "One of them has followed us. Talk later."

Jared repocketed his phone and disappeared.

Samson saw the beam from a flashlight headed in the direction of the treehouse. Samson slipped under the sofa and cloaked the device, hoping the police officer wouldn't poke around under the couch and feel the device even if he couldn't see it.

Footsteps headed up the wooden ladder, the steps creaking as the policeman climbed higher.

The man peered into the treehouse, flashing his light all around the small house. He stared at the sofa, then climbed the rest of the way into the treehouse, the wooden floor creaking with his weight.

"Hey, Joe, this isn't the time to play in a treehouse," a fellow officer joked from down below.

Ignoring his ribbing, Joe crouched to reach the sofa,

then looked underneath, sweeping his flashlight to explore the area. The light in Samson's vision blinded him, and he looked at the floor, maintaining his cloaking ability over the device.

"Nothing here," Joe said, and hurried back down the steps.

The two police officers continued their search and after they moved out of the yard, the device floated out from under the couch, then down the steps as Samson tried to keep up with Jared's running pace.

Once Jared slipped out of the backyard, he sprinted down one street and then another until he was headed in the direction of the river.

Samson figured Hunter would follow them to the river using the demon tracker device and pick them up. So, for a minute, when he saw the device being thrown out over the river, he just stared, unable to move to cloak it or believe what he was seeing. The device hit the water with a splash and sank into the dark water.

He knew Hunter would arrive soon, and sure enough, minutes later, a taxi pulled up at their location. The back door opened as if it had an automatic door opener, and Samson sifted into the back seat. The door shut the same way.

"Mission accomplished," Jared said, appearing in the seat.

"Was that the only device you could find in the house?" Hunter asked.

Samson took his human form and said, "That was it.

The other must have been at the zoo."

"But no one found it, or I'm sure we'd have heard something about it on the news," Alana said.

"So, we still have to locate it." Jared glanced at Samson. "I never thought I'd say this, but we made a pretty good team. I thought for sure the policeman would have found the device under the kid's sofa."

"If he had reached under there, he would have felt it. Maybe he was afraid of sticking his hand in something else."

"What was that?" Hunter asked.

"A gob of spider webs and a nest of spiders."

"Eww," Alana said. "I don't blame him for leaving well enough alone."

"So where to now?" Jared asked.

"The zoo," Hunter said. "The two of you can search the zoo this time. You know more what you're looking for and you can move about undetected."

"The animals will sense us," Samson said. "But yeah. It sounds like it might work."

"Jared?" Hunter said.

"Let's go."

Alana gave the order to the taxi driver, who did as she told him. When they were within a mile of the zoo, she told him to park.

"Couldn't you have gotten a little closer?" Jared asked, but before anyone could say anything, he was out of the taxi.

Samson joined him, and both took on their

clandestine forms, then headed in the direction of the zoo entrance.

"I bet you never expected to be doing stuff like this," Jared said.

Samson reappeared in his human form to talk with his invisible companion. "No. I envisioned staying with Alana always and protecting her from both summoners who thought they had summoned her and from demons that might wish to do her harm. I never expected to be chasing down portal generating devices."

"I have to admit I'd never figured on anyone designing a portal device that not only could be operated from a distance from the lights, but also that could produce several portals at the same time."

"Could you create something like that?" Samson asked, in awe of the genius of such a device.

"I'd never considered building such a thing, but I probably could, given the time and equipment."

"Do you think he had only the two?"

"I hope so. Most likely that's the case. The old version only created one portal. The updated version created several. But you know," Jared said, thoughtfully, "because the other device was close to where the portal showed up, it might not have been far from where the portals appeared at the zoo."

"Old device, remember," Samson said. "This one is much more powerful."

"He might not have even been in the zoo," Jared said. "Then again, Celeste found the fence was cut. The

Matusa wouldn't have done that."

"Celeste," Samson said. "We shouldn't have left her alone at the hotel."

"Don't tell me *you're* beginning to get premonitions."

Samson said, "No, but I didn't think this would take all that long. I just worried that if the Matusa returned to the hotel looking for Alana, he'd find Celeste." Then in more of a hushed tone, Samson said, "We're nearing the zoo."

He shifted into mist and soon he was sifting in through the gates of the zoo as he heard them rattle and figured Jared had just climbed over them.

***

Celeste was watching the news when she heard the metal twisting in the hotel lock. She knew it wasn't the key to the hotel room, which meant only one thing. Someone was trying to break in. She feared it wasn't just a thief, but the Matusa named Thorst who was after Alana.

Celeste quickly hid her demon aura, hoping that would confuse the demon, grabbed the hotel phone, and called 911.

If the Matusa thought she was just a human, he might not mess with her, say his apologies, and leave. But if he had watched any of the news, he might recognize her as the one who had been identified as the girl connected with Alana.

The 911 operator came on the line and Celeste said

in a rushed low voice, "A man's breaking into my hotel room." She gave the location and though the woman told her to stay on the phone, Celeste quickly hung it up, not wanting the demon, if it was a demon, to know the police were on their way.

The door flung open, hit the wall, and before her stood the Matusa. The demon's nearly black eyes stared at her as she stared back at him. Long dark hair curled about his shoulders, and he was taller than she had imagined. Taller than Hunter even, and Hunter was six feet. His face was rugged and hard, but beautiful in an evil way.

The way his eyes grew larger and the way he studied her, she was certain Thorst was surprised to see her in the hotel room instead of Alana. But maybe, too, he was trying to figure out why she would be here. Maybe thinking that Alana had already checked out of the hotel and Celeste was someone new who had just checked in.

He stepped into the room, shut the door with a clunk, and gave her a demonically wicked smile.

She was in trouble. Why couldn't she have some powerful abilities to destroy, rather than future visions that should have warned her of this and allowed her to hide somewhere else for a time until he moved on? But no, she had to learn he was here right as he was picking the lock to the room.

"You are the friend of the one named Alana Fainot, are you not? Though I thought you might be more demonic like her."

That shot down the notion he thought Alana had vacated the room, turned in her key, and was off to parts unknown, and that she didn't know Celeste from Adam.

"Me... demonic? I'm as sweet as they come," she said, still hopeful he thought she was a human friend of Alana's and didn't have any demon abilities—which she didn't if only combat type abilities counted. "We're in classes together at the high school." She spoke most congenially as if she believed he couldn't be a threat to her. "She must have told you we were staying here because of some trouble she's gotten into."

"Ah, still I'm surprised you're not more like her. Then again, maybe not. Finding friends in this world who are more like her would be difficult."

"I've only just moved to the area and met her," Celeste said, hoping the police would arrive before the demon took her somewhere else and forced Hunter and the others to come for her. Then again, maybe the Matusa would just wait for them here. Which gave her a sinking feeling. She didn't have any way to secretly warn them of his arrival.

Car doors slammed outside, and Celeste feared she'd made an awful mistake. Chill bumps erupted on her skin. What if the Matusa killed the policemen? She hadn't even considered that possibility. She had been thinking—break-in, call police, and they'd intervene. Then she realized if the police came, they'd take her in for questioning. If the Matusa didn't kill them all first.

The Matusa parted the window curtain and peered

out, then snorted. "My dear, you have been busy. So you didn't think I was a friend of Alana's after all. Did she tell you about me? Celeste, is it? Perhaps you do possess some demon abilities after all." He glanced back at her. He didn't appear angry, more wickedly amused. Then he glanced around the room as if looking for another way out, but seeing no other way to leave, he moved to the door and opened it, smiling at the police as two approached the door.

Two cars had arrived, but two of the men stayed near their cruiser to serve as backup. The Matusa raised his hands and showed he had no weapons, but Celeste knew he was about to do something deadly.

She hurried past him and slipped between him and the police to protect them. "It's okay. Thorst is my friend. I thought someone was breaking into the room. But I was mistaken. He's fine. Everything's okay."

One of the policemen was communicating to someone else on a phone. "We've got Celeste Sweetwater at the Sunflower Hotel. She's the one who called in the 911. The man with her she called Thorst. He doesn't look like either of the two men she and Alana Fainot had been seen with."

The police officer closest to the Matusa said, "Keep your hands where I can see them. But carefully, bring out some ID. Both of you."

Her purse was in the hotel room, but she wasn't about to willingly confirm who she was. She doubted the Matusa had any human kind of ID. This wasn't going to work. The Matusa wouldn't allow himself to be taken into custody.

"Is that your police car?" Thorst asked. His words were said agreeably, but she heard the dark intent behind them.

The men didn't say anything, but then the one said again in a commanding tone, "Let's see some ID."

The demon's eyes shifted again to the car, his hands still raised and then as if the ball of fire had suddenly sprung from his fingertips, he directed the compact web of flames at the car. The fireball hurdled toward the vehicle. Before it hit, he grabbed Celeste's arm, and she let out a startled shriek. He dragged her back into the room as the policemen dove for cover.

The fireball slammed into the car, hitting the gas tank, and the vehicle exploded. Heat and metal flew everywhere, the fender and part of the roof of the car shattering the hotel window.

Glass shards flew into the room, slicing through her arm, the second explosion knocking her off her feet and onto the floor as a thunderous boom reverberated, shaking the whole hotel.

But what had become of the Matusa? And what did he plan next?

***

Policemen and women were conversing and searching as they looked for the device that had transmitted Alana's image at the zoo while Jared tried to systematically move from one exhibit to another, attempting to locate the portal device.

Because Samson couldn't see Jared in his invisible form and Jared hadn't seen any mist for some time, he realized he'd lost him. Occasionally, he thought he saw a mist somewhere off in the distance, but then he wasn't sure.

All of a sudden, policemen and women were on their cell phones, looking stunned, and then they headed for the zoo exit.

Something had to have happened. Something drastic enough that everyone was pulled off this job. Which had to be pretty high priority. So what had happened?

Police officers were running and clearing the place, and Jared got the sickening feeling the police had located Hunter and Alana who had to still be sitting in the taxi.

"Hell, what's going on?" one policeman said to another as they headed for the exit.

"I don't believe in extraterrestrials, but I'm beginning to rethink my position on the subject."

Had to be Alana and Hunter. What was Jared supposed to do now? Part of him wanted to return to the taxi and come to their aid in any way that he could. Part of him reminded himself that this was his job and he had to look for the portal device, then destroy it if he could. But that didn't keep him from second guessing if he was doing the right or wrong thing.

He finally reached the reptile house, but found no evidence of a portal device anywhere around the building. Yet the summoner had been murdered here. He had to have had either the device with him or had a remote controller. The first one to have come in contact with him was the Matusa. Did Thorst have the remote controller?

Who had the brother been who had picked up Al Cesierone's personal effects? Probably whoever it had been, he was somewhat knowledgeable of Al's electronic devices. But they had no clue who he could have been.

Then Jared had it. If he could access the morgue's security camera tape, they could at least learn what the man had looked like.

A portal appeared a hundred or so feet from him, and he stared at it in disbelief. If he could find the operator of the remote control, maybe whoever it was knew where the device was also.

To his further shock, Alana appeared near the portal in her astral body. Which meant if she and Hunter were in trouble with the police, had been picked up by them even, she was now in her zombie form.

Jared wanted her to know he was here. Wanted to ask her what was happening, but he didn't want anyone to see him if the man now serving as summoner was watching the portal, hidden from Jared's view.

But Jared had to speak with her, so he ran toward her and appeared before her. "Alana."

"Oh, Jared, what's happening?" She looked frantically around at the zoo.

He grabbed her hand, surprised that she felt solid

and real. "The police tore out of here like some major catastrophe had occurred. I was worried about you and Hunter."

"No. It has nothing to do with us. Check your phone for the news."

Jared checked the news and swore under his breath. "Explosion in the parking lot of our hotel. No other details as of yet."

"Celeste." Then Alana frowned. "Why is the portal here?"

"Unless Samson found the device and turned it on, I suspect 'the brother' is here operating the device. And he may have seen us."

"Great." Alana closed the portal. "Terrific. He just opened another."

"Where?"

But Alana had already vanished. Jared concealed himself and ran in a circle, looking to see if he could spy any spin of the portal lights.

He ran one way and then another, unable to locate any sign of them.

"You're a warlock!" Alana screamed from the direction of the giraffe enclosure, and Jared knew she was trying to warn him where the summoner was.

He ran in that direction and saw the guy, a mop of blond curly hair and clear blue eyes, wearing blue jeans and a T-shirt with a scary demon-like winged creature on it. Jared wondered if the dude looked anything like the dead summoner.

"You're a witch! I thought Al had crossed some sort of other world with his portal device," the blond guy said, sounding angered. "But all he got was some meddling witch. So his devices didn't work after all, and you've just messed with our minds, right? Then what? You had your boyfriend kill him? Or did you do the job yourself? So that you can create a national sensation, making people believe that demons live among us? Or, I should say aliens, since that's what the paranormal gurus are saying."

"What was he trying to do?" Alana asked, totally calm.

"Summon demons, of course." He acted like she was an idiot for even asking the question. "Once he summoned them, we would control them."

"What if you could actually summon one? You think some jock warlock is going to control a powerful, evil demon?"

Jared was standing in invisible silence, waiting for Alana to give him a clue as to what she wanted him to do. He knew in her astral body, she couldn't use her powers to fight the warlock. Nor could he hurt her.

Then a wet cold mist brushed against him. Samson was in place, too. He wasn't sure how much he could help while in his misty form, but Jared was glad he was here, just in case.

"Where is the portal device?" she asked, as if he'd just reveal it to her when Jared was pretty sure the warlock had no intention of letting her live. Well, maybe he would let her see it for that reason.

The guy smiled in a smug way. "Wouldn't you like to know?"

"Sure. Why not let me see it? Maybe we can be a team."

"Ha! You're on the national news, witch. I wouldn't want my name to be associated with yours."

"You lied about being the summoner's brother."

"Yeah. But we went way back." He frowned. "I don't remember you being in our school."

"Home schooled."

"Not usually done, but all right. Though I heard you were at the local high school. No witch or warlock would attend a regular school. Why have they connected you with that place?"

"Got me mixed up with someone else, I imagine. So where's that portal device?"

He motioned in the direction of the gorilla cages. "Too bad we couldn't work together. But you're bad news."

"You're not?"

A glint of malice appeared in his eyes. "Maybe you could come with me, and you can tell me how you managed the disappearing act."

"I entered the demon world. Would you like to see it? Just open a portal."

He smiled, the look as demonic as any demon could make. "Oh, sure, as long as you come with me as my guide."

He pressed a button on a transmitter that looked like a cell phone. A portal appeared brighter than Jared had ever seen. Alana waved. "Go right ahead."

"You first."

"Together," she said.

Jared remembered what had happened to some of the demons that had tried to enter the portal into Earth world. They had died.

When the warlock grabbed her wrist and jerked her toward the portal, Jared slugged the man in the face. He lost his grip on Alana, staring in the direction Jared stood. Jared was posed invisibly to strike him again, but the man fell backward into the portal, yelling in surprise.

That's when Jared saw the misty form of a body crouched behind the warlock, which had tripped up the creep.

Just as the portal began to dim and collapse, a stream of shimmering golden energy shot toward Alana and as if it could grab her, dragged her into the vortex.

The portal vanished.

"Damn it to Hades and back!" Jared yelled. Then he stared at where the opening had been and frowned. Her astral self couldn't have been pulled into the portal. Could it have?

He felt frozen in place, unsure what to do. Alana had to be back with her physical form. He wanted to look for the device, but he couldn't, not without knowing if Alana was safely with Hunter in the taxi. But he couldn't open a portal to bring her astral form here to ensure she was safe. Even if he could, he would risk allowing the warlock to return to the zoo.

Samson appeared in his human form and said, "I'll return to the taxi and see if she's in one piece or not. You look for the device."

Jared shook his head. "I run faster than you move in your mist form."

"Well, go then! What are you waiting for?"

"I'm off." At that, Jared ran as if the demons from hell were after him and when he reached the taxi, gasping for breath, he didn't see any sign of either Hunter or Alana. He cursed under his breath and ran back to where he'd left Samson.

To his surprise when he returned, he saw Samson, visible, speaking with Alana.

"What happened to you? I thought you'd been dragged into the portal," Jared said to Alana, highly irritated with her, unable to hide his anger or concern. "If you'd gone through that portal, you could have died." And Hunter would have killed Jared for not saving her.

"I'm not really here, Jared. Remember? Astral self? Besides, I superimposed a portal over his. Mine worked. His might not have. When he fell into the demon world, his portal collapsed, but he would have arrived safe and sound through my portal."

"No, wait," Jared said. "You were sucked into the portal. You were gone. Vanished. Disappeared. Not here." He grabbed her arm and his hand went right through her.

She stared at it, mouth agape.

"You were solid before when you astral surfed." He looked up from her arm to her face. "Alana, what's happened?"

"You know how things keep changing with me." She motioned to where the portal had been and said, "If it's storming as bad as when we were there last, the warlock's soaking wet, chilled to the bone, and scared witless for all his bravado. And he isn't getting out of there unless someone opens a portal to let him back in here." She gave Jared a wicked smile.

He was reminded that she wasn't all Kubiteron demon that were known to be beautiful inside and out. She had a wickedly witchy side to her also, and he hated to admit just how much that side of her appealed to him also. Especially since Hunter was so fascinated with her, and Jared knew he didn't stand a chance.

"Or he knows how to summon a portal in the normal way other than through a mechanical device. But also, that remote controller might operate the device from the demon world," Jared said.

"Highly doubtful. He'd be back here pronto, don't you think? Not only that, but I doubt that the transmitter would work that far away. The portals only opened in the zoo somewhere close to where the device is." She looked in the direction of the gorilla exhibit. "Let's look for that device."

If anyone had told Jared he would have been attempting to break into the cages where the gorillas were housed, he would have told them he or she was insane. But here he was, using his lock picks to try and get into the cage housing a bunch of man-sized monkeys.

"I ran to the taxi, but neither you nor Hunter was there," he said. When she didn't answer, he looked back at her, but her form was fading in and out as if she couldn't hold it together. "What's wrong with you, Alana?"

"Go," she said. "We need to find that device."

As soon as the door creaked open, he moved into the cage, his heart pounding against his ribs. He was invisible, but it was if they could see him, or smell him maybe, and they began to raise a ruckus.

Some of the apes were pounding on their chests, standing upright to show off their height and bulk, attempting to look imposing and vicious. And succeeding.

Oh, sure, Jared knew that gorillas were not normally aggressive toward humans, but shy and retiring. But these were afraid of him, of something they couldn't see. Of something that might not have even smelled all human. Several of the male gorillas roared at him. Some screamed. Others huddled together away from the perceived threat.

He was supposed to be looking for a device. Had the warlock lied about it being here? Hoping they'd look for it and not find it? Jared's attention was focused on the angry apes. He couldn't concentrate on searching for the device when the gorillas were concentrating on him.

If the summoner had managed to hide the device in here, how would he have gotten past the apes?

Then Alana moved into the cage. Instantly, Jared didn't like it. Even though he knew they couldn't hurt her, he couldn't help feeling like they could.

"Alana, stay out."

She stared at where his voice was coming from and frowned. "You haven't moved but a foot into the cage. How are you supposed to find the device if you don't search for it?"

"They sense me. Smell me. They're highly agitated. And they can hurt me if I get close, even if they can't see me."

"Okay. I forget that when you're invisible, you're still physically very much here. I'll go."

"No."

"They can't hurt me, Jared. I'll be fine. If I locate the device, I'll let you know and then you can retrieve it."

She began to move around the outskirts of the enclosure and though he wanted to stay beside her, he knew that if they attacked, they couldn't hurt her astral version. It didn't make him any less leery of the process. He began to move away from her and though they concentrated mostly on her because they could see her, several glanced in his direction because they could still smell him.

He moved quickly now, trying to locate the device so Alana and he didn't have to disturb the gorillas too much. One of the males protecting his family moved toward Alana and Jared couldn't help himself. He hurried to intervene.

Instead of getting in Alana's way, he grabbed hold of her arm, felt its solid form, to his relief, and yanked her out of the gorilla's path. She shrieked. "Jared!"

"Yeah, yeah, you can thank me later." Jared headed for the gorilla and that's when he saw the device sitting inside a tunnel to the indoor exhibit.

"Thanking you wasn't what I had in mind," she retorted.

"If you beat on me," he said, "Hunter will think you have the hots for me, and then where will you be?"

"Where are you going?" she asked as he ran for the tunnel.

"The device is right…" He grabbed it up and held it high. "…here."

Without warning, the big male gorilla swung around and lunged at Jared. He dropped the device and dodged the beast. Since the ape couldn't see him, Jared feinted left and the beast dove right.

Then a mist appeared near the gorilla and the animal lifted its nose and smelled the air, getting a whiff of Samson, Jared figured. Jared seized the device and ran for the door to the exhibit.

"Come on, Samson, Alana!" Jared hollered, running out of the exhibit.

Alana hadn't followed him and instead shouted, "Samson!"

Jared turned, saw the gorilla bite Samson as he threw his arms up in self-defense in his fully visible form. Blood dripped from his arm and then he turned into mist again and melted away.

Jared stared at the place where he'd been. Alana didn't move.

"Alana, come on!" Jared called out. "I'll help him. Just get out of there."

He tossed the device out of the enclosure and heard someone shout, "The voices were coming from the gorilla enclosure."

Jared cursed under his breath.

That's when he saw blood dripping on the ground and the blood trail exited the enclosure. "He's out," Jared said to Alana. "Go. Let Hunter know we're on our way."

He wished Alana could take the device and leave with it so he could help Samson.

That's when he saw Hunter running toward them with the physical Alana in tow. "Something's wrong with Alana," Hunter said, his voice hot with concern.

Jared glanced back at her astral version just as it dissolved into thin air. "The portal," Jared said. "A warlock dragged her astral form into the demon world."

But people, police or zoo staff, were growing closer to Jared's location.

Hunter swore. "All right, you and Samson return to the taxi since no one can see you. Alana and I will go to the demon world." Hunter opened a portal, dragged the unresponsive Alana with him into the glowing lights, but

Jared wasn't about to be left behind and jumped in with him, bumping into a thick mist and smiled.

Samson was with them also.

CHAPTER 10

Debris flew into the hotel room through the open doorway and window after the Matusa sent the fireball crashing into the patrol car. Heat seared the air as Celeste struggled to her feet after being knocked unconscious for precious seconds. Blood dripped from her right arm and sharp pain sliced through the nerve endings. Dizzy and nauseated, she collapsed on the mattress and looked for the Matusa, fearing his next move. Thorst was lying on his back on the floor, a glass shard penetrating his chest, blood pooling around the site, soaking his shirt, dripping on the carpeted floor. He looked worn out and unable to retaliate further, which totally shocked her.

"What kind of demon are you?" he rasped, his face pale, eyes narrowed.

He thought she had injured *him*? He was the one who had made the police cruiser explode, which sent the metal flying into the glass and broke it into a million jagged knives.

"I'm a Camaran demon, a seeker of danger," she said, lifting her chin, relating what Jared had said her demon type was notorious for, although she still hadn't really thought she was that much of a daredevil. She revealed her demon aura.

"Camaran," he said, staring at her for a second, then closing his eyes, he reached for the shard of glass. He didn't remove it, and instead, let his hand fall back to the floor.

She expected him to jerk the glass out of his heart and toss the remnant aside. Then he'd rise and glower at her before he incinerated her. He'd heal himself quickly, then kill the policemen and countless others gathering in the parking lot for daring to cause him trouble.

But he wasn't moving. Wasn't removing the glass weapon. Wasn't healing as she watched the blood collect around the wound.

Seeing her puzzled expression, he smiled in a purely maniacal way. "You have gravely wounded me, Camaran. Your blood is toxic to mine."

In disbelief, she stared at him. She had no combative abilities that she knew of. No defensive ones either. Certainly nothing to use to fight a great Matusa demon.

"Is it only lethal to Matusa demons?" she asked.

"In the beginning," he rasped, "a Matusa and a Camaran loved one another, but when he threw her away for a Kubiteron, the Camaran sought revenge. She begged the god of vengeance to give her a way to destroy any Matusa who might ever desire a Camaran demon."

"No," she said, not believing in some old demon mythology.

"Any Camaran demon so wronged would only have to shed their blood on a Matusa's open wound and that would kill the Matusa."

"You did the damage," she said, feeling even more lightheaded as she grasped her own bloody wound. She needed to get to the bathroom to grab a towel to apply against the wound, but she couldn't gather the strength to head in that direction. Not only that, but the demon was sprawled across the pathway to the bathroom, and she was sure he'd grab her leg if she tried to get past him.

She had to leave. She could do nothing for the demon. She had to get away from here before the police took her into custody.

That's when she felt the air chill several degrees and shivered. She was losing way too much blood. No, her breath was frosting in the air as a white mist. *Indigo.*

Car doors slammed outside, and she heard running footfalls. Her heart slammed into her ribs. More police. They were coming for her now.

She looked back at the Matusa. He was staring up at the ceiling as if not truly seeing.

"You killed the man at the zoo, using snake poison, didn't you?" she asked, hoping that she might get a confession of sorts from the demon in case the police could hear them speaking. She saw shadows near the doorway and thought a policeman or two were listening.

If they questioned the demon before he died, she was certain he wouldn't tell them anything. But maybe she could help Alana and herself out of this mess if he would answer her question.

The demon snorted. "He deserved it. No one summons one of my kind without paying for his or her actions."

"So you killed the man in the reptile house. Did he beg for mercy, Thorst?"

"He was stupid and fearful. How he thought he could use our kind and…" The Matusa gasped for breath. "He deserved to die."

"You threatened Alana. Tried to grab her and take her with you." Celeste had to give a reason why Alana had tried to hide from the police and this dangerous man.

"She would… have been mine." Thorst coughed up blood.

"She's safe," Celeste said, frowning at him. "Safe from the likes of you."

The Matusa smiled bitterly. "She would have been safe from anyone had she returned with me." He closed his eyes and shuddered, then took his last breath.

She watched him for what seemed like forever until she was sure he had died. Then she lay back on the mattress and closed her own eyes. So tired. If only she could escape to the demon world.

Running footsteps headed for the door. Men shouted orders. Sirens blared while the fire outside still raged.

The slice in her arm hurt so bad, she was certain

somehow the Matusa had poisoned her also.

Then she saw men in SWAT uniforms dash into the room, guns readied before all the lights turned dark inside her head.

***

Hunter and Alana arrived in the demon world where the storm they had been through had abated, though gray thunderheads still blanketed the sky and lightning flashed in the distance. The torrential winds were still blowing the waves against the bulkhead near the city, threatening to breach the massive stone wall. What really got his attention was a tall blond-haired man, who was holding Alana's astral self against his chest, threatening her bodily harm if a group of six Matusa didn't back off.

Other demon types watched from a distance as if fascinated by the entertainment, but not moving close enough to get involved.

Hunter felt smug-satisfaction to be holding the physical Alana close to him while the Matusa thought they might have a chance at her astral form.

"Let go of the Kubiteron, human, and we'll let you live," one of the Matusa said to the man holding Alana's astral form, but Hunter knew better.

If the man released her, the Matusa would annihilate him.

What the demons didn't know was that the Alana the human was keeping hostage was only her astral self.

As soon as the portal lights caught everyone's attention, they all turned to look in Hunter and Alana's direction. One of the demons was Tarn's brother.

They all looked back at the human holding Alana's astral form as if trying to figure out what was happening. Then as if the proverbial light bulb turned on, one exclaimed, "The Kubiteron is a gate guard!"

Alana's astral form vanished, and Hunter knew she'd reconnected with her physical form as she suddenly looked alarmed and threw her hands up to create a water spell, sending a wall of water crashing into the demons. Before any of the demons could regain their footing and make a move toward Hunter and Alana, he pulled her into the portal and closed it.

And tripped over two bodies that he couldn't see. "Hell, Samson, Jared, I told you to return to the taxi. What if you missed coming back with us?"

But then he and Alana were dodging behind buildings, attempting to get out of the zoo before anyone discovered them.

Jared said, "We were there in case you needed help."

Hunter hmpfed. "The only one who needed any help was that stupid human who dared take Alana's astral form into the demon world and then held her hostage. He's definitely dead meat now that he doesn't have her to shield himself from the Matusa."

"He was a warlock. He might keep them off him for a while, but as many as there were, not for long, I imagine," Alana said.

Hunter smiled down at her. "I'm sure they all have the hots for you now that you smashed them with a wall of water."

She shrugged. "Someone had to put them in their place. I bet the warlock wishes now that he had never messed with our kind."

Jared said, "To think he believed you only to be a meddling witch."

Alana smiled, and Hunter wrapped his arm around her shoulder. She was *his* meddling witch, but he didn't like that her astral form could now be pulled through a portal.

"What happened anyway?" he asked.

"She covered his portal with her own because his version wasn't stable," Jared said. "Then he pulled her astral body through the portal by casting some kind of electromagnetic field. I saw another version of her astral self here, but it kept fading in and out as if she couldn't maintain both astral versions. Of course, when I saw her, I thought there was just something screwy about this astral form, not believing she could have another one in the demon world."

"Yeah," Alana said. "Now I have to be in three places at once? No way can I be stable in all three places."

Hunter didn't say anything for a minute, fighting a smile, then Jared laughed. Hunter cast him an irritated look and Jared said, "I'm not touching that comment. Really."

Before long, they'd managed to get beyond the zoo and were running flat out for the taxi. But it was gone.

Alana grabbed her cell phone and called for another taxi while Hunter incinerated the portal device. Black metal melted all over the asphalt road. That was the end of the summoners' portal devices.

Now all they needed to do was return for Celeste and take care of the Matusa, wherever he was. When they arrived in the taxi at the hotel, they found police everywhere, a patrol car burning out of control as firefighters tried to put out the flames and a very pale Camaran demon on a stretcher was carried out as medical personnel hurried her to a waiting ambulance.

She had to be all right. Demons had great regenerating abilities. But she looked like she wasn't all right at all. They would follow her ambulance to the hospital, and he'd send Jared in to check on her. His gaze shifted to a body bag as others carried out someone who had not been as fortunate.

This has all been the work of the Matusa. Hunter would bet his life on it. Where was the bastard now?

"Samson's wounded," Jared said, when the Samuria demon wouldn't let anyone know about it.

Hunter frowned. "Samson, make yourself visible."

He did, clutching his arm, his face showing pain, but also annoyance. "It'll go away."

Alana shook her head and made him remove his shirt, then tied it over the bite marks. "Maybe we ought to get you a tetanus shot."

"Maybe one for the gorilla," Hunter said.

Samson shook his head. "It's already healing. It just

looks worse than it feels."

From Samson's expression, it looked like the injury felt worse than it looked. Hunter nodded and said, "It's nothing more than a scratch."

Everyone looked at Hunter as if he was crazy. He gave them an elusive smile. "Just think if it had been a Matusa who had clawed him."

That put the whole injury in perspective. Hunter had nearly died from such a wound and no matter what recuperative abilities demons had, fighting that poison on his own had not been an option.

Alana put her hand over Samson's injury, closed her eyes, and chanted. Hunter knew she was helping the demon to heal faster, so why did he want to jerk her hand off the Samuria who looked at her as if she was his guardian angel... and his chosen mate?

With her heart in her throat, Alana finished healing Samson to the extent she could, then watched out the taxi window with the others. Indigo leaned against the waiting ambulance as medical personnel carried Celeste into it. Indigo saluted Alana, then climbed into the ambulance. Surprised that he'd been here, she wondered if he'd tried to protect Celeste. She couldn't help but admire the ghostly Matusa for joining Celeste when she'd been all alone.

Alana knew that Celeste would pull through because of her demon genetics, but she couldn't help worrying about her and what she was in for next.

"She'll be all right," Hunter said, squeezing Alana's

hand reassuringly.

"Until they question her."

"The Matusa?" Jared asked, hopefully as they watched the body in the bag go into another vehicle.

"We shouldn't have left her here alone," Samson said.

"Follow the ambulance. Jared can slip in and see her and learn what's happened," Hunter said.

The police were so busy cordoning off the area and searching for clues as to what had happened, that none of them noticed Alana and the others watching the scene along with countless others.

Alana directed the taxi driver to the hospital, and when they arrived, Samson wanted to go with Jared. But Hunter said no. "Jared can move around unseen. He can talk to her if she's awake. But you appear in the form of a mist, Samson, and in the hospital, it would be a trifle odd."

Indigo was suddenly sitting between Jared and Samson, smiling. "She'sss going to be okay," he said.

"What happened?" Alana asked the ghostly Matusa.

Hunter said, "What, Alana?"

"I'm talking to Indigo."

Hunter grunted.

"She'sss smart. She made him confessss. One of the policemen wasss taking notesss outside the hotel. Another wasss recording the conversssation. They'll know she wasssn't involved. That you weren't, either."

Alana couldn't give a sigh of relief. She wasn't sure

anyone was convinced of their innocence yet. "What about the Matusa?" she asked Indigo.

"Dead. She killed him."

Alana conveyed what Indigo had said, "The Matusa is dead. Celeste killed him."

Jared swore under his breath. "Nothing in my demon stats says anything about the Camaran demon that indicates they have combative abilities."

Indigo sneered at him. "Showsss what you know, Elantusss."

Alana was glad no one could see the ghost or hear him speaking. "How did she kill him?"

"Her blood, of course," Indigo said.

"Blood?"

"Not only doesss it act asss an anti-coagulant, it'sss poison to a Matusa'sss blood."

"All Camaran's blood?" Alana asked, shocked to hear it.

"Oh yesss. Deadly to a Matusa. They don't take Camaran for their matesss. Too dangerousss."

Alana closed her gaping mouth. Everyone was waiting for her to relay the news, whatever it was, and she took a deep breath and said, "Indigo says that the police officers got the Matusa's confession."

Hunter shook his head. "I would never have thought one would tell what happened."

"He didn't give one to the police," Alana said. "Celeste was smart enough to get it out of him. The police were outside the hotel room, taking notes, probably waiting for the SWAT to arrive."

"Okay, that sounds more reasonable," Hunter said. "The Matusa would have left everything in total chaos if he could have. What about the Camaran's blood?"

"Deadly to a Matusa," she said.

Jared began typing the notes into his database on demon types. "How is it deadly?"

"Poisoned and also it won't allow the blood to coagulate."

"Bleeds until he's dead. Remember that Hunter," Jared said, typing away.

When they arrived at the hospital, Jared went inside. Indigo slipped inside also, and she wondered if he could actually see Jared in his invisible form. Even so, Jared couldn't see the ghostly Matusa.

She wished she could go with them and offer Celeste moral support. As tense as Hunter was, she knew he hated being left behind, too.

All they could do was wait and see.

***

In the operating room, Jared watched the surgeon sew muscle and tendons back together again and reconnect arteries and nerves where Celeste had been injured. Fascinated, he wondered if maybe he should be a doctor.

Celeste looked sweet and innocent like an angel, but pale as death.

The room was cold, but even more so now, and Jared wondered if Indigo was with him.

The surgery seemed to take forever, then Celeste was wheeled into a recovery room where Jared watched over her. She appeared to be sleeping, though he leaned over to give her moral support and whispered in her ear, "Celeste, we're all here for you."

Her eyelids fluttered open and she shivered, staring up at him with half-lidded eyes.

"Jared," she whispered.

He squeezed her icy hand and said, "Yeah, in the flesh. Well, invisible flesh. I don't want to shake up the nurse."

"What happened?"

"You killed Thorst, apparently. At least that's what Indigo said. If he's to be trusted."

Chilly air cloaked Jared. "Indigo's here also, watching over you."

Celeste tried to smile, but though the effort was valiant, she could barely force the curve to her lips.

"Rest," he whispered. "Hunter and the others are waiting outside, dying to see you."

"The devices," she said in a raspy voice.

"Destroyed. Samson and I tossed one in the river. On the way over here, Hunter incinerated the second device. He can make them melt into a pile of metal goo or turn paper into fine ash. He's very good at it. He can do it without igniting anything in the vicinity or underneath the targeted object. He was always destroying summoner books that way. But of course, this is a little different."

"Alana."

"She wants to see you. Everyone does. Even Samson." Jared turned to see a strange mist settle next to the bed. "Hell, Samson, what if someone had seen you? And you're injured yourself. You're supposed to be resting in the taxi." Then he frowned at Celeste. "I had no idea what you were capable of. Just don't get mad at Hunter and try anything."

She let out a shallow breath. "I suppose you added that to your demon database."

"Absolutely. Not that I'd forget what you're capable of, but for future reference in case any clueless demons, like us, need to know. Anything else we need to know about?"

She gave him an annoyed look. He smiled.

"What happened to Samson?" she asked.

"Got bitten. It doesn't pay to make a gorilla go ape."

"Are you okay, Samson?"

"He'll heal. Like all of us will. Alana helped the healing process also. She would have helped you also if she could have before you were brought here. Do you want me to get you anything?"

"Just a way out of here," she said, and he squeezed her hand again, and whispered, "Soon."

After an hour, she was wheeled into another room. There, two police officers came in to see her, and Jared wanted to throw them out on their ears. Celeste looked the worst for wear still, her skin pale while she received blood, her eyes barely open.

"Celeste Sweetwater," one of the men said, "do you mind if we ask you some questions?"

She shook her head.

"What were you doing in the hotel room where you were injured?"

"Hiding from Thorst," she said, her voice soft.

"From Thorst."

"The man who killed the one at the zoo."

"How did you know about Thorst's involvement in the killing?"

"I see future events in visions. I saw what he had done."

The policemen exchanged looks that said they believed in psychic abilities as much as they believed in the Loch Ness monster.

"So, you saw this man killing the other in a vision, but why would you be hiding from him if he couldn't have known you knew about him?"

She let out her breath in a heavy sigh as if annoyed that she'd have to explain what any imbecile could see. "I tried to stop him. Okay?"

Now the men stared at her with incredulous expressions.

"Stop him, how?" the one asked.

"I went to the zoo. He saw me, but I realized then I couldn't stop him. I had forgotten my cell phone so I couldn't call the police. I slipped out the way I had come."

"Then you must have seen Alana Fainot. She was

there and had witnessed the murder."

"I don't know if she saw him or not. She... experiences blackouts. She was worried about me and followed me to the zoo. Then, I left, figuring she'd leave, too. But... I guess she was still in one of her states and didn't leave when I did. You picked her up and questioned her. I was afraid to come in to talk to the police, knowing Thorst would try to kill me for having witnessed the murder."

"What exactly did you see?"

Jared couldn't believe it as Celeste explained exactly what she'd seen when the Matusa had killed the summoner. They were taking fastidious notes, one questioning her, then the other. He assumed they'd check every detail and learn that everything she said had truly happened. He admired her for having seen all and was a viable witness, of sorts.

"Why did this Thorst kill the other man?"

She shrugged, then grimaced. "They both were a little crazy. Thorst wanted the device the other had made. He thought he was creating a portal device that could allow demons to be summoned to this world, and then he'd control the demon. Thorst thought the device might work and wanted it, too. How stupid could they both be? No one can do such a thing. The blue-green lights were like a magician's showy effects."

"You disappeared into them. We saw you," the one policeman said.

She waved her good arm dismissively. "Part of

Thorst's theatrics. Some kind of optical illusion. Camera tricks." Then she frowned and looked from one to the other of the men. "You don't really believe a portal can open to a demon world, do you?"

***

As they sat in the taxi in the hospital parking lot the day after Celeste had been injured, waiting for Jared to return with news of her release, although he'd noted that Samson had slipped out also, Hunter contemplated moving Alana to somewhere else other than Baltimore. She didn't need to be in school. Couldn't be if she was going to continue to have the trouble with controlling her problem with being called to portals when they suddenly appeared.

Before Celeste was ready to leave the hospital, Alana insisted on visiting her and Hunter wasn't letting Alana go anywhere on her own. When they reached the lobby, two policemen stopped her at the door.

"Alana Fainot, we need to talk with you."

Hunter was ready to open a portal and drag her into the demon world, but Alana tugged him with her toward the lobby and said, "Sure. What did you want to know?"

Hunter hoped when they'd questioned Celeste, her story and Alana's would be the same.

The men introduced themselves and she smiled and said, "Yes, I remember you both from before."

She introduced Hunter and the men looked like they were remembering her earlier testimony.

"The guy who went with her to Holiday World,"

Detective Ryker said. "Let me see your ID."

When Hunter handed it over, the detective frowned, then raised a brow at him. "She's underage, you know."

"We just rode some rides, officer," Hunter said.

The man didn't look like he believed Hunter, but they all moved toward the lobby area in silence.

Once they were seated in the waiting area, the harder-looking detective said, "Where did you go when you disappeared from the lady's room at the police station, Alana?"

"I left. I knew that the... Thorst would track me down. So I hid at the hotel."

"With his help?" the detective asked, motioning to Hunter.

"No," she said. "Samson dropped me off at the hotel."

"Samson. The guy from your class."

"Yes."

"And you stayed there until?"

"I went out to get pizza."

"With this Samson?"

"Samson had left earlier. Hunter came by and picked me up and we went out for pizza."

"Where's Samson?"

"I don't know where he went to."

"There were no pizza boxes in the hotel room."

"We heard the explosion before we reached the pizza place and returned, worried about Celeste. Then we saw the patrol car on fire. We waited until we saw

Celeste was on the stretcher and followed her to the hospital. We heard she was leaving today."

"So, you came to see her. What do you know about Thorst?"

"I don't know anything about him."

"Why did you go to the zoo?"

"You asked me before. I said I went to see the lions."

Detective Ryker cleared his throat. "Did you have something to do with the other man? The one Thorst murdered?"

"No. I didn't know either of them."

"What do you know about Celeste's... visions?"

"Pretty cool, don't you think?"

Detective Ryker looked hard at her. "Nothing adds up. How you got to the zoo. Why you were really there. How you got out of the police station without anyone seeing you. How you left the parking lot at the hospital, vanishing in thin air." He paused. "Some kind of electronic device was stolen at the murdered man's home. Do you know anything about it?"

"No. Why should I? I didn't know him. Don't know where he lives. Haven't any clue what he was doing."

"I believe that you know a lot more than you're letting on, Alana." He closed his notebook, rose, and shoved the book in his pocket. "If you remember anything further, let us know, won't you?"

"Absolutely," she said, getting to her feet.

Hunter stood beside her.

Detective Ryker said to Hunter, "Stay out of

trouble." Then he and his partner left the hospital.

Alana sighed with relief. "Hopefully since they got their man, they'll leave us out of it."

Hunter escorted her into the elevator. "I was afraid I'd have to open a portal and start the speculation all over again."

When they reached Celeste's floor and found her room, she was already dressed and ready to leave the hospital. She smiled brightly at them. "I'm being released today and going back to school tomorrow. Will you be there?" She looked hopeful.

Hunter didn't want to allow Alana to go.

Alana took Celeste's hand and squeezed it. "Yeah. What's one more school year among friends?" Hunter opened his mouth to speak, but Alana said, "Jared told me you said he and you were enrolling in school with us."

"That was before you were on the news," Hunter said caustically.

"Yeah, well, you can take care of me." Alana patted his chest, smiling up at him, looking purely demonic.

And he loved it.

"All right. But any more trouble like this, and we're going somewhere that no one knows us."

"All right," she said and slipped her hand around his.

He pulled her tight against him and wrapped his arm around her waist, looking down at her. "I choose the classes we'll be in. No calculus, for one."

"No argument there, but Samson will probably not

like it."

"Samson doesn't have to like it."

Alana said, "How are your foster parents dealing with all this, Celeste?"

Celeste shrugged. "I'm bound for another foster home. They couldn't handle all this bad publicity. They figure because of my visions, it's not going to get any better."

"Do you want to come home with us? My mother's a witch, but in a good way."

Celeste frowned. "She wouldn't mind? Really?"

"Oh, no, you'll fit in fine."

Samson shifted from mist into his human form and said to Celeste, "I'll stay with you in calculus class. Help you out if you need any."

Celeste's expression brightened. "I'd love that. Thanks."

Jared made himself visible and scowled. "We graduated last year. I can't believe you want to do this, Hunter."

"Someone's got to take my girl to the prom," Hunter said. "And it's going to be me."

Both Samson and Jared looked at each other, then at Celeste and smiled.

Alana said, "Indigo offered to take you, Celeste. He said he'd never messed with a Camaran demon before, but because your blood can't hurt him now, he's game."

"He's a ghost," Jared said, sounding annoyed.

"She'll go with me," Samson said.

Jared crossed his arms. "She'll decide." For the first time, Jared's eyes glowed red over a girl.

Hunter couldn't help but smirk at him. Time would tell what happened come the prom. For now, it was time to take Celeste home to Alana's house.

"Ready to go home?" Alana asked.

"Not before I learned I could live with you, but now I'm loving the idea. Whatever happened to the warlock who got stuck in the demon world?"

"For a while, the Matusa will undoubtedly want him to open a portal. If he can't, they'll either kill him or let him flounder. Other demons might not like him though, knowing he might have intended to bring one of them through to Earth world to be his slave," Alana said. "If he's smart, he'll act clueless, although I'm certain they'll want to know how he ended up in their world. He'll have fun explaining that."

"Hipalon demons will know the truth," Jared said.

Everyone looked at him. Hunter recalled what Jared had said about their type, though they'd never encountered one.

Jared explained, "They always know if someone's telling the truth or not. They use them as investigators in crimes. So if they want to know the truth, they'll call on one of the Hipalon."

"Did the police talk to you, Alana?" Celeste asked.

"Yeah. Unless more portals open and someone catches sight of them or we're linked to more dead bodies, I'm sure we'll be fine."

"Do you think you might want to go with me to the hall of records in the demon world sometime?" Jared asked Celeste.

Samson didn't look pleased. Celeste smiled wistfully up at him as she sat down in a wheelchair, the only way the hospital staff would let her leave here.

"You know, maybe someday we could do that."

Before Alana could say anything, Hunter said, "No, you're not going with her."

Trying to get Alana away from there the first time she went had been dangerous enough. Samson looked torn. He was supposed to protect Alana, never leaving her side. But he looked like he didn't care for the suggestion that Jared would take Celeste by himself to the demon world.

Hunter grunted. He was not going to let them sway him to allow Alana to go with them, and he wasn't leaving her behind to protect the others, either.

Alana took his hand as Samson wheeled Celeste out of the hospital room. "We'll all go."

"It's too dangerous for you," Hunter said, expecting his word to be obeyed.

Samson jumped in. "Yeah, we'll all go."

"I'm the Matusa here."

As cold as he suddenly felt, Indigo must have tried to let him know he was here, too.

"What is Indigo saying?" Hunter asked Alana.

She smiled. "He'll help you protect me. Which means come spring break, we'll all go."

Hunter let out his breath and wrapped his arm around Alana's shoulder and kept her close. "You remember what happened last time?"

"Yeah, you saved us."

He shook his head, knowing he wasn't winning this battle. When other kids were getting in trouble at sunny resorts all over the world, he was going to be trying to protect a bunch of demon friends in Seplichus. Not exactly what he'd had in mind when he had become a demon guardian for Earth world.

He sighed heavily. What the heck. He was a Matusa. If Alana wanted to help Celeste find her real parents, and Jared discover where his were, too, Hunter would be right there with them. Maybe he'd even learn more about his brother that his demon father didn't want him to meet.

Hunter straightened. His father wouldn't like it, but Hunter's half-brother had every right knowing what he truly was. Maybe he could help him cope a bit.

He looked down at Alana as they waited in the lobby with Celeste and Samson while Jared went to get a taxi. "I don't want you going, you know. I want to remind you in case you've forgotten, you are mine."

She laughed. "You know, Hunter, you're so arrogant."

"Yeah, and you love me for it."

She sighed and snuggled closer. "Will you be getting an apartment in the area?"

"Condo, if Jared's parents will swing for it. If not

right next door to your mother's place because none are available, somewhere else in the complex nearby. You need watching because of this portal business. Until you can control your astral self—"

"I know, I know. I'm trouble."

He smiled down at her, loving Alana just the way she was. "Yeah, my kind of trouble. We'll try to find something out about my brother while we're in the demon world this time."

Alana looked up at him with wide eyes. "Oh, Hunter, yes."

"And we'll see your father if we can locate him."

She nodded, smiling enthusiastically.

"And Indigo, maybe we can convince him to stay there."

Alana glanced to her left, then said to Hunter, "He said he's staying with us, so get used to the idea."

"It was a long shot."

A taxi drove up, and Jared came back inside as Samson began to wheel Celeste to the vehicle.

"Did I miss anything?" Jared asked no one in particular.

Celeste said, "Just that Hunter's going to look for his half-brother while in Seplichus, too."

Jared stared at Hunter, then shook his head. "Ha, I thought only Camaran demons had death wishes."

Then they were off to Alana's house, condo buying for Jared, school the next day, and a spring break venture that could lead them into all kinds of danger. The kind of peril only demons like the six of them could get into.

For now, Hunter wanted to take Alana on a real date.

Without everyone else tagging along.

"Wanna go eat, then see a movie later?" Hunter asked Alana.

That got a round of "yes" responses from everyone.

Alana laughed. "Yeah, I'd like to go, too."

That would be their first official date. Surrounded by demons of all kinds and a ghostly Matusa, too. But it wouldn't always be like that, Hunter vowed.

ABOUT THE AUTHOR

Bestselling and award-winning author **Terry Spear** has written over sixty paranormal romance novels and seven medieval Highland historical romances. Her first werewolf romance, *Heart of the Wolf*, was named a 2008 *Publishers Weekly*'s Best Book of the Year, and her subsequent titles have garnered high praise and hit the *USA Today* bestseller list. A retired officer of the U.S. Army Reserves, Terry lives in Spring, Texas, where she is working on her next werewolf romance, continuing her new series about shapeshifting jaguars, writing Highland medieval romance, and having fun with her young adult novels. When she's not writing, she's photographing everything that catches her eye, making teddy bears, and playing with her Havanese puppies. For more information, please visit www.terryspear.com, or follow her on Twitter, @TerrySpear. She is also on Facebook at http://www.facebook.com/terry.spear. And on Wordpress at:

Terry Spear's Shifters

http://terryspear.wordpress.com/

Follow her for new releases and book deals: www.bookbub.com/authors/terry-spear

http://terryspear.wordpress.com/

ALSO BY TERRY SPEAR

Young Adult Titles:

The World of Fae:
The Dark Fae
The Deadly Fae
The Winged Fae
The Ancient Fae
Dragon Fae
Hawk Fae
Phantom Fae
Golden Fae
Falcon Fae
Woodland Fae (TBA)

The World of Elf:
The Shadow Elf
The Darkland Elf (TBA)

Blood Moon Series:
Kiss of the Vampire
Blood of the Vampire (TBA)
Night of the Vampire (TBA)

Demon Guardian Series:
The Trouble with Demons
Demon Trouble, Too

Demon Hunter

Non-Series for Now:
Ghostly Liaisons
The Beast Within
Courtly Masquerade
Deidre's Secret

The Magic of Inherian:
The Scepter of Salvation
The Mage of Monrovia
Emerald Isle of Mists (TBA)

Adult Titles:

Romantic Suspense: Deadly Fortunes, In the Dead of the Night, Relative Danger, Bound by Danger
The Highlanders Series: His Wild Highland Lass, Vexing the Highlander, Winning the Highlander's Heart, The Accidental Highland Hero, Highland Rake, Taming the Wild Highlander, The Highlander, Her Highland Hero, The Viking's Highland Lass, My Highlander
Other historical romances: Lady Caroline & the Egotistical Earl, A Ghost of a Chance at Love
Heart of the Wolf Series: Heart of the Wolf, Destiny of the Wolf, To Tempt the Wolf, Legend of the White Wolf, Seduced by the Wolf, Wolf Fever, Heart of the Highland Wolf, Dreaming of the Wolf, A SEAL in Wolf's Clothing, A Howl for a Highlander, A Highland Werewolf Wedding, A SEAL Wolf Christmas, Silence of the Wolf, Hero of a Highland Wolf, A Highland Wolf Christmas, A SEAL Wolf Hunting; A Silver Wolf

187

Christmas, A SEAL Wolf in Too Deep, Alpha Wolf Need Not Apply, A Billionaire in Wolf's Clothing

White Wolf: Legend of the White Wolf, Dreaming of a White Wolf Christmas, Flight of the White Wolf

SEAL Wolves: To Tempt the Wolf, A SEAL in Wolf's Clothing, A SEAL Wolf Christmas; SEAL Wolf Hunting, SEAL Wolf in Too Deep

Silver Bros Wolves: Destiny of the Wolf, Wolf Fever, Dreaming of the Wolf, Silence of the Wolf; A Silver Wolf Christmas, Alpha Wolf Need Not Apply, All's Fair in Love and Wolf

Highland Wolves: Heart of the Highland Wolf, A Howl for a Highlander, A Highland Werewolf Wedding, Hero of a Highland Wolf, A Highland Wolf Christmas

Billionaire in Wolf's Clothing, A Billionaire Wolf for Christmas

Demon Hunter

Demon Guardians

Book 3

TERRY SPEAR

DEDICATION

Thanks to Janice Bolick, who loves my stories and follows me on Goodreads! May you have the best of times always!

ACKNOWLEDGMENTS

Thanks to all my fans who have waited so patiently
for the third book in the Demon Guardian Series!
.

ABOUT DEMON HUNTER:

Hunter is half a Matusa demon, determined to help his human-raised demon friends return to the demon world to find their families. And to help Alana learn a way to keep portals from pulling her to them, and getting herself into all kinds of trouble. Not that she can't handle some of the trouble on her own. She's a half demon too, and half witch. Jared is looking for his parents. Celeste is looking for hers. Samson is there to protect Alana, though Hunter keeps reminding him Alana is his to protect.

It was a simple mission, but nothing for the demon guardians is ever simple. Between dealing with a demon who is organizing demon hunters—who go after Hunter and his friends, a major train wreck, and all sorts of havoc, it's no wonder the demon gate guardians end up calling in reinforcements this time.

As long as Hunter can get Alana to agree to be his mate, he can save the world. Alana will never give up her hot demon, but she believes he should work a little harder to prove he is the one for her. And he's not going to give up trying to convince her either. But they still have one little problem: staying alive long enough to do it

CHAPTER 1

When other seniors in high school were thinking about spring break and all the trouble they could get into south of the border, Alana Fainot and her demon friends were planning the hot-spot destination of Seplichus—and the search for other demons. Specifically, their friend Celeste Sweetwwater's kin—her summoner parents having been murdered by a Matusa when she was just a three-years-old, so she didn't know who her real parents were—Jared's parents, Alana's father, and Hunter's half-brother.

Three more days and they could go to the hall of records and hopefully locate everyone they needed to.

"Omigod, he is the hottest thing ever," a blond-haired girl said to another, eyeing Hunter as he made another boy move from his seat in Alana's English class, so he could sit next to Alana and watch over her.

Alana rolled her eyes at him. *She* was a total demon magnet because of her Kubiteron demon kind, but Hunter was a total human girl magnet. He was a half-Matusa demon, one of the evil kind, though Hunter's human half tempered his demon half.

Alana couldn't believe how bold the girls were when they were nearby, making sure he heard just how interested they were in him. Alana couldn't deny the attraction she had for him and the annoyance she felt for him. Yet she loved working with him, when she didn't want to kill him. He was a Matusa, after all, and that meant he was arrogant and stubborn to a fault.

Well-muscled because of his karate training to fight the evil ones and send them back to their world, he was totally hot. He was dark-haired and dark-eyed, just like she liked guys, his hair shaggy, bad-boy look, perfect.

It didn't matter one iota that Hunter stuck close to Alana as much as he could, worried about her being pulled to an opening demon portal. If the human girls could do neat tricks like that, maybe *they* could have garnered his interest.

He glanced at her, gave her a small smile, and she was certain it was because he wanted her to know she was lucky to have him….according to the human girls. Or maybe he was just amused that they were interested in him, and it annoyed her. Though she was trying not to let it show.

Before she could say something to wipe that smug smile off his face—Indigo moved in between them. The ghostly Matusa demon was torn between wanting to haunt the students in the classroom that she was in *or* that Celeste Sweetwater was in—another one of their demon friends thrown together with them due to the strange events of the past year—and their group was fast becoming a melting pot of demon gate guardians. Their purpose: keep the Matusa demons from entering Earth world, and returning any of the demons that people summoned into their world to Seplichus.

Hunter growled low under his breath, "Get lost, Matusa."

Hunter didn't like that any other demon would try to come between him and Alana. Even if the demon was merely a ghost. But Indigo was a *full* Matusa demon, and he felt that Alana *was* his. So did Hunter, despite being only half demon.

"Admit it," Alana whispered to Hunter, "he's one of us now. We'd miss him if he wasn't on our team."

Hunter grunted.

Indigo had helped them so many times when facing the danger of the Matusa demons, they really owed him their lives.

At the end of the period, the teacher gave out their reading assignments. When they left the class, Jared rushed to meet them at their lockers. Jared had been fighting demons with Hunter for a number of years already. His dark hair was wind-blown, his amber eyes narrowed, and he was trying to catch his breath. He was the computer geek of the bunch, always coming up with cool new gadgets to help them in their quest. "Have I mentioned how dumb it is for us to return to high school?"

"Daily," Hunter said, exchanging books at his wall locker.

"Yeah, well"—Jared waved his demon monitor tracker, the size of a cell phone at him—"my tracker picked up activity at the Jiffy Ice Cream Shop. How are we going to just leave the school to check it out?"

"What kind of demon?" Hunter asked, frowning.

A blond-haired girl and her dark-haired girlfriend moved closer and said, "Oooh, are you into summoning demons?"

Jared tucked his demon tracker II device into his pocket, while Alana and Hunter scowled at the girls.

"You mean, like a video game?" Hunter asked, growling a little.

They couldn't believe how the Matusa demons were infiltrating their world, via being summoned. Once one was here, he'd encourage more summonings. No one could ever be sure what kind of demon they summoned either, until they were there. Strictly humans didn't know there was a grand difference between demon kind. To some though, it was just a game. They didn't really believe messing with summoning spells would bring any demon to their world. If they called a Matusa, they'd be dead before they realized summoning demons wasn't a game.

The girl pulled some books out of the locker near Hunter's. "Summoning demons in a video game? Of course not. We heard you talking before about demons, and we wondered if you're into that role-playing game."

"What role-playing game?" Hunter asked, sounding annoyed, but concerned also.

Even if it was some lame game they were playing, they always had to take any mention of demons seriously.

Alana was worried too. Summoning demons could be really bad news for everyone. They couldn't dismiss that the girls might be talking about something that was for real.

Any hint of demon summoning activity and the demon guardians were on it. They had to be. They owed it to their kind—both on this side and in Seplichus, the demon world. The humans, or at least most of them, were clueless.

"Well, it's a secret, so if you're not into demons," the blond said, shrugging.

"Oh we're *very* much into demons," Jared said, who was a full Elantus demon, no human blood at all. "What is the game all about?"

***

Tonight, they had to scope out the extra-curricular activities of the self-professed, demon hunters, but for now, Hunter and Jared slipped out of school to check on the demon at the ice cream shop, while Alana protested that she wanted to come also. But *she* had to graduate from high school. Hunter and Jared had already graduated, had diplomas, and were just pretending to need their senior year at Alana's high school to watch over her. Celeste was in the same boat, needing another year of high school to earn her diploma, but she was taking another class for now, though she was a couple of years older them. Moving from one school to another because of moving from one foster family to another had been the problem for her. And, well, skipping school.

With a stern word to Samson, Alana's self-proclaimed gate guardian guard—Hunter had told him to watch over her at all costs. Alana was supposed to be a gate guardian, and Samson, as a Samuria demon, claimed to be her guard and her intended mate, which neither Alana or Hunter bought into. Samson wasn't even of this world, so he definitely didn't need any human schooling, but he sure was good at it, Hunter had to admit.

Hunter hoped Alana would stay put. He didn't trust her one little bit. But once he'd assured himself that she wasn't going anywhere—the demon having already being summoned, apparently, so there would be no portal opening that would pull Alana's astral form to it—he and Jared took off for the ice cream shop.

"Are you certain your demon tracker is accurately showing the demon type?" Hunter asked Jared.

"Yeah, Celeste's kind of demon. A Camaran demon."

"Then it's probably her signature you're seeing. Did you try to reach Celeste on her cell phone and make sure she's not skipping classes again?"

"Yes, and she must have her cell phone turned off. I haven't been able to get ahold of her."

"But she, or whoever the Camaran demon is, is still at the ice cream shop."

Jared glanced down at the tracker that he had built himself. He was a whiz at stuff like that. "Yeah."

"What about tracking Celeste at school?"

"She hides her demon aura. So I don't know if she's at school or not. She kind of blinks on and off sometimes. I swear it's to annoy me."

Hunter smiled. Demon types were like that.

"I see Alana's Kubiteron demon type in class, Samson's Samuria signature, sitting next to her. Then you and me in your vehicle driving—" Jared paused as he glanced at the shop as they passed it by. "Hey, Hunter, you just passed the ice cream shop."

"Matusa demon is straight ahead."

"Uh... wait, my demon tracker shows that's a Camaran. How did he, oh, he's running."

"He must be one of the kinds who can mask his demon type. For a moment, he shed his Camaran masking, and I saw his true demon type."

"Does he know we're following him?"

"I don't think so. He has to have been here a while if he didn't just come through a portal or Alana would have been pulled to it."

All of a sudden, the demon whipped around, stared hard at Hunter, then turned his attention to Jared, and back to Hunter. And grinned.

"Hold on tight. We're in for trouble," Hunter said, trying to make a corner, the car's tires squealing, before the Matusa blasted them out of existence.

Note to Reader:

Thanks so much for reading my Demon Trouble Too!! I hope you have enjoyed the excerpt for Demon Hunter! Lots more demon trouble to come!

Terry Spear

http://terryspear.wordpress.com/

Made in the USA
Monee, IL
16 October 2020